LAS VEGAS BOOTLEGGER

LAS VEGAS BOOTLEGGER

Empire of Self-Importance

by Noah Cicero

Trident Press
Boulder, CO

ISBN: 978-1-951226-07-7

Edited and Typset by Nathaniel Kennon Perkins
Cover art: Detail from *Home of the Desert Rat* by Maynard Dixon
Author Photo: Vi Khi Nao

Published by Trident Press
940 Pearl St.
Boulder, CO 80302
tridentcafe.com/trident-press

"I see the goodness in you, but I'm not fuckin' with it."

— *Prof/Rail Yard Ghosts*

NOTICE!

Dear Reader,

This is not a book of polemics. I do not share the opinions of the characters in this book. This book was not written on behalf of any political, religious, and/or ideological institution/idea.

This is not a novel. This is fiction, as in the stories described in this book do not depict events that can be historically validated as factual. Even though this book stretches to an extensive amount of pages, this does not make it a novel. Novels have much more coherence on average than the story depicted in the following pages. If it is called a novel, it is only for the purposes of marketing and shelving.

If you expect to open this book and find a well-written novel in the style taught by Master of Fine Arts programs, please either put the book down, or at least let me help you. This book is closer in spirit to Plato's Dialogues, Dostoevsky, and Kathy Acker.

This book was written during July 2020, in the middle of a pandemic.

Sincerely,

Noah Cicero

Chapter 1

Ryan Neroni, Las Vegas personal injury attorney, stood in the kitchen of his modest four bedroom house in Summerlin, Las Vegas. His mother Margaret was finishing cleaning the dishes. They had lived together going on six years.

Ryan was 39 years old in the year 2019. He grew up in the 90s. His childhood was mildly annoying but not PTSD inducing. His father was a workaholic who spent ten to 12 hours at the office every day. When Ryan's father did talk to him, it was never playful. He was always serious. Even when Ryan was five years old his father spoke in long compound sentences to him. All of his father's friends were professionals who were just as serious, they had serious lives, they all had similar houses, similar cars, similar wives, and it was all serious. They were the type of men who wore suits, the type of men who spoke perfect English, and who had favorite sports teams. These men did not work on cars or build sheds in their backyards or mow their own grass. They were not millionaires, just middle class. Ryan found his place in this world. He was sent to the best Catholic schools in the city of Las Vegas, he consistently had straight A's. Everyone remarked on how well spoken and smart he was, how handsome, how Margaret (his mother) had a lovely child. Ryan believed he was well spoken, believed he was smart, and believed he was handsome. When Ryan was in high school he continued to achieve straight A's. He learned Spanish and took every advanced placement class the school offered. Ryan fed off the adoration of adults, he believed that adults were a path to success, he had no reason not to believe them, at no point did he feel upset by how adults treated him. After he would bring his report card home, his mother, an RN, would give him a powerful hug, she would kiss him on the cheek and tell him she loved him. It was true, Margaret loved Ryan with all of her heart. She would bring him to any store he wanted and let him pick out over 100 dollars worth of things at the local mall if he received all A's. Ryan would pick out books, clothes, and new shoes. While Margaret and Ryan walked the malls, she would walk close to Ryan, often touching his shoulder and smiling. Ryan loved when his mother smiled at him. He truly wanted to make her happy. They were happy together as they walked through the mall. Ryan's father would also supply benefits in regards to Ryan's perfect grades, the father would tell him he loved him and that he was proud of him, then they would go to a fancy restaurant and have a big dinner. His father would talk about work and give monologues about business and the financial world. Ryan would listen and nod. Ryan did not know that at the same time, other children his age were never being told by their parents that they were proud of them, that some children were being beaten and had drug addicted and violent family members, that some children had immigrant parents who spoke different languages and could not help their kids study, and that they did not receive delicious meals, regardless of how good or bad they did in school. Ryan did not know. He assumed everyone had a similar life to his. Ryan went to college and continued his habit of attaining great grades and impressing adults. His college life was not full of partying or amazing sex. He would sometimes get drunk on Saturday night. One night he was stumbling home from a party, and he decided in his intoxication to urinate on the side of the road. A cop stopped his car and asked him what he was doing. Ryan immediately apologized. The cop offered to drive him back to his dorm. Ryan had never been in a cop car and felt excited by it, he felt safe with the cop. The cop made jokes about getting drunk and told him to be more cautious about where he peed. Ryan heeded his advice and no longer peed on the side of the road. Ryan was peacefully left in front of his dorm. College came easy to Ryan, he could read the professors and figure out what they expected of him. Ryan's major was political science. If the professor was an old white Republican, he would gear his opinions in that way, if the professor was a middle-aged liberal African-American concerned with social justice, he would shift his opinions that way. He could make arguments, that was his talent, he could easily adjust his manners, personality and entire philosophy to endear the adults around him. When Ryan finished his undergraduate degree he was able to receive recommendation letters from the most stubborn old white Republican in the department and from a young Latino Woman who was devoutly liberal. No one had ever achieved that before.

Ryan scored an LSAT score of 174, which allowed him to go to the University of Chicago. Everyone was proud of Ryan when this happened. His whole family threw a giant party, relatives and family friends came, there were meal trays, and many of his father's friends, some of whom were lawyers, came and spoke to Ryan, in a serious tone, as one complete man to the beginnings of a man becoming complete. Ryan soaked all of this in, it filled his heart full of joy to know that the adults that he had believed in since he was a child, now, after 23 years, finally and totally believed, that he too, was going to become a true adult, a serious man, a man to be taken seriously, a man that would be part of the community, an important person among other important people.

Ryan went to law school. As usual, it went splendidly. Ryan did what he was supposed to do, he learned the law, he passed all the tests, and he became a lawyer. He missed his mother though and went back to Las Vegas to become a personal injury attorney.

Ryan began his career. As before, it went swimmingly. He started at a smaller law firm and worked his way up, receiving amazing settlements, one after another. Eventually they started letting him do trials, and when he could win he won, and the ones he lost, there were legitimate reasons why he lost. He wasn't a rainmaker, but he was sturdy and dependable. No one really liked him, but they trusted him. Five years ago, Ryan landed a job at the top personal injury law firm in Las Vegas, at Bernstein Biviano. Mr. Bernstein was incredibly successful, owning a giant Roman style house in Floyd Mayweather's neighborhood in Summerlin. Mr. Bernstein was a king of Las Vegas, his law firm had repeatedly won cases for over 100 million dollars. Every powerful person in Las Vegas had his number in their phone. Ryan worked as he always worked, he impressed Mr. Bernstein, he tried to impress Mr. Biviano, but Mr. Biviano lived in his own strange world and had no time for anyone. Mr.

Bernstein often brought Ryan into his office, and just like Ryan's father, he would give long monologues about business and sports. Ryan was happy that he had endeared himself to Mr. Bernstein. It was a great source of pride.

Margaret had lived for Ryan since the day he was born, she was a knight for Ryan, she had carried many crosses silently for Ryan. Margaret woke up and went to work at the hospital and in recent years at a rehabilitation facility for wounds, broken bones, burns, amputations, and strokes. At the hospital where Margaret worked when Ryan was younger, she had many cruel doctors and annoying fellow employees. She wanted to walk away from her job so many times, but she remained agreeable for Ryan. She did all this silently, crying in her car on the way home and not in the house in front of Ryan. Margaret found comfort in the local Catholic church where she went two to three times a week. She would attend Sunday Mass, a meeting on Monday, usually on a specific book of the Bible, and on Wednesday she would sponsor new Catholics at an RCIA (Rites of Christian Initiation for Adults) class. When there was a bake sale or any such event, she would help out. She would give blood every three months. Sometimes on Saturday she would volunteer at Catholic Charities, helping the homeless. Ryan would sometimes attend Mass on Sunday morning, maybe once a month. He had enjoyed the music and the ceremony since he was a child, and he knew it made his mother happy.

MARGARET: We have a five hundred and fifty pound patient at work.
RYAN: What?
MARGARET: He is five hundred and fifty pounds.
RYAN: (*Looking puzzled.*)
MARGARET: The doctor told him, "We are going to get you special shoes to walk." The five hundred and fifty-pound man looked at her and said, "I don't walk." Then the doctor said, "What do you mean you don't walk?" The five hundred and fifty-pound man said, "I haven't walked in eleven years." The doctor looked at me and I looked at the doctor, we were confused by this confession. The doctor said, "Why haven't you walked in eleven years, is there something wrong

with your legs?" The five hundred and fifty-pound man said, "No, one day, I laid down in bed and decided to never get up again." The doctor said, "Never? Like it was a life-choice?" The five hundred and fifty-pound man said, "Yes." The doctor persisted, "But what, instigated this choice?" He replied, "I was done." The doctor said, "Done with what?" The five hundred and fifty-pound man said, "Done." The five hundred and fifty-pound man looked at her like she was stupid, then he looked at me like the doctor was crazy. The five hundred and fifty-pound man truly had no idea why this was important.

RYAN: How does he live?

MARGARET: His sister takes care of him. She even wipes his ass every day.

RYAN: Wait, oh yeah, he just poops himself doesn't he?

MARGARET: Yes, just poops himself, he has been pooping himself for eleven years.

RYAN: Does he take showers?

MARGARET: He gets wiped off with washcloths.

RYAN: (*Staring blankly, vacantly.*)

MARGARET: Well, now he can't walk. All of his muscle tone in his legs is gone. If he stood up and walked, his legs would break.

RYAN: How old is he?

MARGARET: Fifty-five. I've seen bigger, but they could always walk. Some people are just big, but this is different.

RYAN: Do you think he is mentally ill?

MARGARET: I assume he is mentally ill, but what the problem is I do not know. I don't know what led him to make the decision to never stand up again. It has never occurred to me once to never stand up again, it seems inconceivable. I remember when your father and I got divorced, I felt very crushed, not because he was leaving, he could leave (*She chuckled*), but that I had put so much effort into something and it failed. I wanted to lay down forever, just wither away, and for a week, I did lay in bed. As I lay there, I remember distinctly feeling that I did not understand how the world worked, that I had failed a test, that I did not prepare properly and I must be immensely stupid for having put myself into this situation at all. Feeling stupid is the worst feeling, the feeling of distrust of oneself, of losing all confidence in one's decision making faculties. There is nothing worse than that in terms of moods one may have. I assume that eleven years ago the five hundred and fifty-pound man had lost all confidence, but what made him lose it, he probably doesn't even know, and if he knew, he wouldn't trust that he knew it.

RYAN: There is this legal term, *res ipsa loquitur*, it is like, when an elevator drops suddenly and injures people, at the scene of the accident no one knows what caused the elevator to drop, but something must have happened, but we won't find out till much later, after an investigation has been done. It is like that man is *res ipsa loquitur*, you look at him and know something must have happened, but what and when?

MARGARET: It takes three of us to hold him so we can clean his butt.

RYAN: I don't understand how he lives. Yet he lives. He never wants to kill himself?

MARGARET: He seems completely satisfied with his state of affairs.

RYAN: How does he live though?

MARGARET: (*Laughing.*) Ryan, everything lives. You are judging him referencing your own values and personal experience. Cats and dogs live, all the animals in the desert live, trees and plants live, it doesn't take a lot to live.

RYAN: (*Confusion.*) I don't understand, how can something just live? How does a five hundred and fifty-pound man live, doesn't he want...

MARGARET: Want what?

RYAN: Want, you know, to achieve things?

MARGARET: (*She looked thoughtful.*) Maybe he doesn't want...

RYAN: What doesn't he want?

MARGARET: To participate I guess.

Ryan had never questioned the nature of participation. This was new to him, he thought of what his co-lawyers and his father would say, the 550 pound man was lazy, a no good piece of shit, a shiftless useless asshole, etc. Ryan wanted to say those things, but it seemed like his mother did not hold that viewpoint, which meant Ryan could not hold that viewpoint.

Margaret started talking about something else, how one of the nurses didn't call a doctor, etc.

Chapter 2

Shortly after speaking with his mom regarding the 550 pound man, Ryan went outside to sit by his pool. Almost every night at 9:30 p.m., Ryan sat in a reclining chair and drank a kombucha to settle his gastric reflux, which caused halitosis. Since his early 20s, he had had bad breath. Ryan did everything he could to control his gastric reflux, he took pills, he chewed on Tums, he carried gum and breath mints everywhere. If he knew he was going to have to speak to someone up close, within three feet, he would have anxiety, not crippling anxiety, but anxiety nonetheless. He would set an alarm on his phone alerting him of when he had to chew gum. If he neglected to freshen his breath there was an annoying voice in the back of his head notifying him that everyone could smell his breath. He did whole depositions with this voice in his head, the voice would not end until he went out to his car and was driving home. This is the main reason he was not married, his bad breath. To be an unmarried male personal injury attorney was a social crime. If you were a woman, no one cared. Women had their code and men had their code. He knew every male personal injury attorney, Plaintiff and Defense, was married. They were always married to other professionals, doctors, administrators, psychologists, etc., or to a housewife, but the housewife came from "a good family," and had at least a bachelor's degree. Ryan had never been married. He'd never come close to even asking a person to marry him. He hadn't even dated a woman in ten years. After his halitosis came into his life, women remarked, not in a rude manner, but regardless Ryan always took it personally, they said, "Your breath smells really bad. I don't want to kiss." This would make Ryan very upset. He wouldn't scream or yell, he would simply apologize, then never speak to them again. After it happened a third time, he drove home in tears. It was one of the few times in his life, a disability had come to restrict his movements. He didn't understand why such a dumb issue had arisen in his life, he didn't understand why there was not medical treatment that could resolve the issue. Ryan stubbornly decided never to date anyone again, to put the idea out of his mind. If he considered it, if he met a woman he liked, he just told himself, "No, you cannot do that, please stop thinking these thoughts." He was very lucky though. After dating websites and apps became popular, people from his generation no longer flirted in public. People could be people now. Sexual tension was a thing of the past. If someone wanted sexual tension they could go online and pick from a variety of people, go on a date with them, watch *Game of Thrones*, and have sexual tension. If a man behaved, never mentioned sex, never did anything creepy, he would never have a sexual moment in his entire day. Not dating anyone eventually led to skin hunger, the lack of human touch that led to feelings of depression, a sense of loss, and spells of anxiety that would last for weeks. Ryan did not know that these physical and mental developments were linked to his skin hunger. The phenomena was inexplicable to him, and he would never approach this subject with friends because he knew that objectively he had no real friends, and those unreal friends did not care. He couldn't tell his mother because he did not want to worry her. Every night he went to sleep alone, he would have preferred if someone was there, but he didn't understand why.

As Ryan drank his kombucha he remembered a year back when he interviewed a client that was at the October 1st Shooting. This was Ryan's first big case, the biggest mass shooting in American history. On October 1, 2017, on the Strip in Las Vegas, a man named Stephen Paddock shot into a concert, killing 58 people and injuring many more. Las Vegas had never seen such an event. Las Vegas was part of no wars. No plague had ever entered its city gates. The worst thing that ever happened in Las Vegas was the MGM fire of 1980, killing 85 people. People believed that Las Vegas was a safe place for people to gamble and commit venial sins.

One of Ryan's jobs regarding the October 1st Shooting case was to collect people's stories of what happened that night. Ryan had heard one horrifying story after another. In general, they were all the same, people seeing their family members shot, or themselves being shot, and there were also PTSD cases where people saw people get shot and it caused psychological issues that led to them missing work and having to attend a therapist. The PTSD people were different from the shot stories, those who were shot and those who saw family members shot stayed where they were, but the PTSD people were able to leave and enter into other locations. Everyone that night was thrust into a night of chaos and pandemonium, the world of the real, where the reality of television and entertainment and all that they were taught about life meant nothing. Something real was happening. Uncertainty was at level ten for one night in many people's lives.

Ryan interviewed the client in a small conference room. Ryan was sitting with his suit jacket off, with a small notebook in front of him. The client, Jordan Merton, was sitting across from him. Jordan was in his late 20s. He had on a baseball cap with sunglasses on the brim. He wore a t-shirt and blue jeans, and he drove a large truck. Jordan worked in a casino doing maintenance, and he had never missed a day of work. He had a Facebook page with pictures of his wife, one child, a dog, and his truck.

Ryan looked at this man across from him, perplexed at how this man's life turned out so differently from his. They were both white, they were both male, they were both approximately the same age. Two very different sets of masculinity had ruled their personal codes. Ryan wanted to look at him and justify his life. He either wanted to declare to himself that he made a mistake in life or that this man made a mistake in life. He did not know how both modes of masculinity could be right or favorable or true. Of course younger people didn't believe in either version of their masculinities.

Jordan told Ryan about when he first heard the shots, he made the same sound everyone else did, "pop pop pop." At first he thought it was fireworks. Then, when Jason Aldean left the stage, he knew something was wrong. Then he saw people being shot and falling to the ground around him. He told how he went through a fence, how he ran up the street. He said he didn't know what happened, that no one knew how many shooters there were, they could have been anywhere, he ran so fast he made it into the Bellagio. He said that doesn't even make sense when looking at a map, but he said, "I ended up there."

JORDAN: You know what was really strange, while everyone was screaming, running in all different directions, there was this man, I think he was wearing a suit, but he had a hiking backpack. The backpack was bright red. That's why I remember it. It was so odd to see a man wearing a nice suit with a backpack. Well, he was walking in the opposite direction than everyone else, he was walking right into it, like he knew he had to get out of there. It was terrifying, I thought maybe he was one of the shooters, and now he was escaping. We learned later that everything would go on lockdown, and somehow this man knew, lockdown and searches would be the inevitable result of the shooting. But like how, how did this man know? It was so weird, in the midst of screaming crying people, there was one man who had no fear, who I assume had to get something illegal out of that area before the police started searching.

Ryan randomly thought about this story, he wanted to know the truth of this man, the man who had a job to do, in the midst of chaos. There was an unknown man in this world, a man who had chosen to do tasks under the cover of night. Ryan had only done his tasks in the light of day. His whole life was a recorded event. He had always dreamed of being a Partner and then becoming a judge. He had done everything right to make these things happen. While he was doing things that could be viewed in the light of day, there was another man that lived a secret life. Ryan never knew a secret life was possible. No one had ever said, "When you grow up you can have a secret life where the tasks of employment occur outside the view of the public. It isn't a public or private life, but a secret life." When Ryan was a teenager, on Saturdays and in the summer months, he would watch movies on TBS and USA, movies like *Smokey and the Bandit*, *White Lightning*, and *Gator*, bootlegger movies. He also watched mafia movies with his father, *Godfather 1* and

2, Goodfellows, and *Casino*. The characters seemed so cool to him, men of other means.

Chapter 3

A few days after the 550 pound man conversation, Ryan Neroni was at work in his office. His office had all of his diplomas and certificates on the wall. A giant wooden desk. The desk was clean and well-kept. There were two chairs in front of his desk, each pointing at him. There was a shelf with a sparse collection of books related to trial methods. There were no novels or poetry or philosophy or books of history on the shelf. Ryan does not remember the last time he read a novel, let alone a poem. He never wondered about his lack of concern for the arts. He had no opinion on the existence of any art. He didn't consider it. He didn't have any friends who considered it.

He received an email from his accountant. Ryan had recently settled the case regarding the October 1st Shooting. It had settled for 700 million dollars. Ryan was entitled to a percentage of that award. Ryan had previously received several percentages of cases' awards. Ryan had put all of these percentages into a structured bank account where the money would grow interest, and instead of collecting all the money at once, money would be deposited monthly into his bank account for several decades. Ryan asked his accountant to calculate, after this new award of millions, what his monthly income would be for the next 30 years.

Ryan saw the email and became excited, as anyone would be, over money. Ryan read the email:

Dear Mr. Neroni,

With the new additional funds added to your previous account, your income will be \$12,546.67 per month for the next 30 years. If you have any questions or require additional information, please do not hesitate to contact our office.

Thank you, Rachel

Ryan felt a deep sense of relief reading the number $12,546.67. He felt secure, like his life could never fall apart. He would always have money. He had made it in life. He would forever be a serious man, just like his father and his father's friends. He was a winner in this world. He had conquered. He had proven that he was a champion of Public Life. He was not worthless. People had found his worth and paid him handsomely for it. He was victorious and no one could take that away from him. The adults had cherished his company and all the hard work was not for nothing. He had an income for the rest of his life. If he wanted to stop working today, he could. Nothing could stop him from walking out of the office and never returning. Then it occurred to him, "I could go home?" Up to that point in life, he was supposed to be dreaming of being a Partner, his own billboard, possibly being a judge. He was still young. He could become a District Court judge and then move on to Appellate. He could become a real name in the pantheon of Las Vegas judicial history. He would have ex law clerks that told stories about him and his quirky ways long after he died. There would be a picture of him in the Regional Justice Center (Clark County Courthouse), in Downtown Las Vegas for as long as Las Vegas lasted on this earth.

He felt conflicted for the first time in his life. This was a new feeling for him. He usually and predictably had the mood of total control. He always knew where his destiny lay, what behaviors he should perform to attain that destiny.

Ryan sat in his chair not working for about 20 minutes, just staring out the window with his hand under his chin. If anyone looked into his office, they would have thought he was contemplating what to write next in a motion. No one would have expected he was "thinking."

Ryan realized he wanted to get bottled water and took a walk to the kitchen area, a small area with a sink, refrigerator, microwave, and coffee maker. On the way there, he heard a noise coming from a small windowless office. A paralegal named Theo was listening to music in his office. Theo had bought special speakers and often listened to music loudly in his office. Theo would play classical music during the day, Bach, Mozart, Chopin, and Mendelssohn, and sometimes he played folk style music. Ryan never listened to music while working. His office was always deathly silent. Ryan had never considered music. It seemed useless to him. His parents never gave him any love for listening to music. People at various times in life asked him what his favorite song was, and he never had a good answer. Eventually they would give up and move on to other subjects.

As he walked through the hallway, he heard music coming from Theo's office, and he didn't understand what was happening. He felt something. This new feeling was difficult, it was shocking, he had to investigate, he was a lawyer, and Theo was a paralegal, he could walk into his office and take up his time. He didn't need to ask.

Ryan went into Theo's windowless office.

RYAN: What is that?

THEO: (*Looked up confused. Why is this lawyer in my office? What does he want? And it is freaking Ryan, that tasteless bastard.*) It is Rail Yard Ghosts, they are like a folk band.

RYAN: Is it a video? May I watch it with you?

THEO: (*This dude is so weird, he creeps me out.*) Okay, no problem. Have a seat.

Ryan sat down, Theo started the video at the beginning. It was Rail Yard Ghosts, "A Month from now, Whatever you Like."

RYAN: They look homeless. Are they okay?

THEO: Yeah, they are crusties.

RYAN: What is a crusty?

THEO: They are people that ride trains and hitchhike. They play folk music with any instruments they can find.

RYAN: They have really dirty fingernails, and it doesn't seem like they get haircuts promptly.

THEO: (*This dude is out of his mind.*) They don't care.

RYAN: Aren't they worried?

THEO: Worried about what? They are beautiful. What is there to worry about?

RYAN: (*He arched closer to the screen. He let himself see these musicians as beautiful.*) Theo, they are beautiful. I see it. Play it again.

THEO: (*Wow, what is happening with this dude? This is interesting. I hope this self-important bitch has a fucking mental breakdown.*)

RYAN: What are they saying? I mean not the words, but I feel like it's saying something, like these strange dirty people are trying to tell me something.

THEO: They are telling you to let go.

RYAN: Let go of what.

THEO: Everything that isn't real.

RYAN: What isn't real?

THEO: I'm not a therapist or a zen master, Mr. Neroni.

RYAN: At four minutes and three seconds she makes a noise. What is that?

Theo played the specified section several times.

RYAN: She looks like shit, but she is so beautiful. A person can be beautiful and still look like shit?

THEO: (*Did not know how to respond.*)

RYAN: Please stop whatever work you are doing, unless it is deadline sensitive, and send me a list of bands via email that are similar to Rail Yard Ghosts.

THEO: Okay.

Ryan walked to Mr. Bernstein's office, he stood outside his door and knocked lightly. Mr. Bernstein asked him to come in, Ryan sat in one of the chairs in front of his giant wooden desk.

Bernstein immediately started talking about the Golden Knights, his season tickets, that he sits next to a famous neurologist and the owner of 20 Mcdonald's franchises. About how defense lawyers are fucking idiots and that we have to shit on their faces, that adjusters are fucking idiots, that this defense law firm is fucking evil and we have to watch out for them, and this other defense firm is full of insurance cocksucking bastards, and all their faces have to be shit on, and we are the good guys, we are fighting against insurance companies on behalf of the little man, and all these defense firms are insurance loving fuckfaces, and their faces need to be fucked because they are stupid. Ryan had no time to speak. Mr. Bernstein talked quickly, without giving openings.

RYAN: Mr. Bernstein.

MR. BERNSTEIN: Yes? Have you considered getting season tickets to Golden Knights games?

RYAN: No. I am resigning.

MR. BERNSTEIN: (*Looking disappointed/angry.*) I don't understand, this is the biggest law firm in Las Vegas. Where will you go? Are you moving? Did someone snatch you from Cali?

RYAN: No, I'm done. I'm done being a lawyer.

MR. BERNSTEIN: I do not understand this, you are on your way to becoming partner in a few years, or even a judge. You have a fucking opportunity to be a judicial legend in this town. This is fucked up, you are throwing away your future. (*Mr. Bernstein was sad.*)

RYAN: I already have enough money to live the rest of my life. I don't see the point of carrying on with this. I have no wife or kids. I'm going home alone every night. I mean, I live with my mom. She has her own money though. She doesn't need any of my money. I don't even feel interested in my own life. I don't even remember it. Does anyone remember me?

MR. BERNSTEIN: (*On his second wife. First wife supplied him three kids. Two of them were on track to becoming successful in the STEM fields. Only one was weird. His second wife was 14 years younger than he was and had amazing fake breasts. When Mr. Bernstein left the office every day, he drove home to two kids who wanted to see him, one that quietly hated him but mostly stayed in her room, and a wife with the eternal breasts of a 15-year-old. Mr. Bernstein left the office feeling great. He absolutely loved his life. It had never occurred to him that Ryan was alone and left the office to no one. Maybe that's why he always came to work on time and left later than his assigned time and he didn't mind taking ridiculously complicated cases. Mr. Bernstein allowed himself to have empathy for approximately 22 seconds, just enough to gain understanding but not really.*) Sigh. Maybe you should go on a dating website.

RYAN: Huh? I quit. This is my decision. This is my last day, I don't care about working out my two weeks. I don't see any need in being here anymore.

MR. BERNSTEIN: I don't understand. You are on your way. No one will look at you anymore and care if you aren't an attorney. You will be another dumbass standing in the grocery line or at a gas station. What job could you possibly do? Here, in this office and at the courthouse, we are kings. We are men to be respected, to be feared. Everyone is complacent to our wants and needs. People don't question us, even if we are obviously wrong. And that, my friend, is true power, to be wrong and treated like you are right.

RYAN: Thank you for everything. (*Ryan stood up and left the office.*)

Chapter 4

Ryan went back to his office and sat at his computer. He opened up an email in Outlook and clicked on the email that sends emails to the entire office. He wrote:

> I am quitting today. This is my last day of ever being an attorney. If anyone would like to come to my office and tell me I'm a piece of shit or that they liked me, you can do that. You can say anything you want to me. Please do not hold back. Regardless of what you say, I will supply a great reference for you.
>
> Thank you for the last five years.

The first person that came to his office was a late 20s African-American woman named Breyonna. She sat across from him.

BREYONNA: I can't believe you. Your whole way of life is unbelievable to me. This is what it is like being around you: so many times I have come to your office, knocked on your door politely, and wanted to ask a little question, and you told me, "I don't have time." I had a question, a real fucking question. I get nervous about doing a good job, I get nervous about getting fired and getting bad reviews. All I ever wanted to do for you is to do a good job, and you don't want to answer my question. I would have to go back to my cubicle not knowing what to do. I would send you an email, hoping you would answer it, praying that maybe an email might be better suited to get the answer I wanted, but no. You didn't even reply to my emails. One time, I had the simplest, dumbest question, and it took five weeks for you to answer it. Five fucking weeks. What kind of behavior is that? One time I knocked on your office door, you told me, "I don't have any time to answer you right now," then Mr. Bernstein walked into your office and you stopped everything you were doing and spoke to him for half an hour. What the fuck is that? Am I human? Were you purposely trying to tear me down psychologically? I am not your fucking flunkie. I'm a fucking person. I understand that Mr. Bernstein is your boss, but to tell me you have no time "for me" but you obviously have "time" for "him." Just because I can't give you promotions, doesn't mean my dignity is something to be dismissed. You have done nothing but dismiss me and my personal wants and needs for the entire three years I've worked here. I used to think it was just me, maybe it was a race thing, a woman thing, but every non-attorney and even younger attorneys were completely dismissed by you. Everything is about your time for you. It is probably why you don't have kids or a wife. You are a time hoarder. You think you own time, you are entitled to time and money, it is all yours, and people like me, well, we get scraps of time and money. Seriously, attorney Eunji supplies all of us with time. You knock on her door, she lets you in, and you can talk for as long as needed to get the job done. If she is really busy, she says, "I'll Microsoft Teams you to come to my office," and in less than an hour you can come to her office and have a chat. You never did that. Everyone loves Eunji. Regarding you, everyone just shrugs their shoulders or flat-out talks shit. You're the kind of person people talk shit about, well-meaning people, not your usual shit-talkers. (*Breyonna looked at him disappointedly.*) This is your legacy here, a man that wouldn't talk to anyone.

RYAN: So my understanding is I hoard time.

BREYONNA: You not only hoard time; you have a hierarchy of who gets your time. Seriously, what is the point of hoarding time? Where are you going? You are here nine hours a day. That is five hundred and forty minutes a day. Even if you just had me come into your office and sit with you while you ate lunch for twenty minutes, we could have chatted and it would have helped the case. Fuck, why am I saying this? You don't think I could help the case. It has never occurred to anyone like you that we are a team or coworkers. You probably sincerely assume that only through your genius do things get done. That the mere fact you trust someone, it isn't their work and personal decisions that move the case along, but "your trust" that is doing all the work. It is hard to believe the lies you attorneys tell yourselves. I mean, does law school have a class called "how to lie to oneself so you can feel important and entitled." Of course, American law schools have been built by successful white people, so I'm sure this is just a recurring subliminal message that teaches you the bullshit matrix. (*Talking in a funny voice.*) Take the red pill and consume yourself with entitlement and hierarchical bullshit. Assume your life is just better, feel insecure at all times about your place in society, make sure to announce to your employees making twelve dollars an hour that you have already saved up enough money to send your kid to Harvard or Yale on their tearfilled work. Take the red pill of insecurity and entitlement. (*Stopped talking in a funny voice.*)

RYAN: No one ever told me I'm insecure.

BREYONNA: Oh my God! Seriously, you are in a constant, unrelenting state of having to make sure that everyone in this temporary social paradigm perceives you as an important lawyer who does important things and makes important decisions, and his decisions revolve around vast sums of money. You never want to be found out. You never want to show vulnerability. Never. You are never vulnerable. Your white masculinity drains us, never for a second showing any vulnerability at all. At least with black masculinity, they are allowed to love music and sometimes break into vulnerability. You can't do that. The white middle-class masculinity has completely consumed you, you would probably have a fucking meltdown if you went longer than ten days without a haircut. If you had to drive a Nissan Versa, a total breakdown of your masculinity.

RYAN: So you are saying my confidence is only a coping mechanism to hide my profound insecurity? My dad and his friends weren't champions of business, the medical and legal world; they were actually deeply insecure men?

BREYONNA: Did you read Ayn Rand in high school? What the fuck is wrong with you? Of course, everyone is insecure. Don't you fucking get it?

RYAN: Everyone is insecure? Everyone? (*This echoed in Ryan's head. He had never thought about everyone. Who was everyone? What did everyone have to do with him? Could everyone have things in common? Natural things? Universal things? He had truly never considered everyone as something worth contemplating. What if he had to write a motion on everyone? What if everyone did have things in common? Maybe not nature, but predicaments. Predicaments of commonality in our personal and private lives.*) Thank you for notifying me of my behavior. I will think deeply about how I hoard time and will try to change my habits. Perhaps I cannot fix the damage I have done to you, but perhaps in the future I will be more apt to not hoard time.

Next came Dana, the receptionist, a middle-aged white woman who Ryan knew nothing about. Ryan had never once held a conversation with her. He'd never avoided her, never thought the sentence, "I'm not going near Dana," but Dana had thought many times, "I hope I never get in a situation where I have to talk with Mr. Neroni."

DANA: Do you remember six months ago when Stacy's friend killed himself, and she wrote on Microsoft Teams to the whole office that her friend killed himself and that we need to stay alert, that one of our friends might be suffering, and we need to talk to them, let them know that we care, and you wrote for the whole office to see, "Yes, that's true. When someone is suffering, we have to lend a hand, we have to show them that we care, even if it is just a friendly text." Do you remember writing that?

RYAN: Yes, I do. (*He actually didn't, had no idea what she was talking about.*)

DANA: Later on that day, less than three hours later, Miki threw her down her keyboard, crying, and yelled, "I can't do this anymore," and walked out of the office. Do you remember that?

RYAN: Yes. (*He didn't remember that either.*)

DANA: Did you text her? Did you try to find out what made her so upset? Did you attempt any communication at all with her?

RYAN: No.

DANA: But you wrote three hours earlier, you have to reach out to people, you have to show concern. You're a liar, you don't fucking care. It was just to show the entire office, a performance, just another pile-of-shit move by a big piece of shit. A few of us girls cared. We texted Miki. We went to her house and ate popcorn and watched a movie. Were you there?

RYAN: Was I where?

DANA: At Miki's house! Can you even name one thing about Miki? She worked ten feet from your office for five years. I bet you didn't even know she had a kid, or what Asian country she was from, never bothered to find out.

RYAN: (*Sorting out which Asian country Miki was from based off her name; concluded it was either Japan or Korea, definitely not China.*)

DANA: At least I have love.

RYAN: What... love? (*The mention of love confused him. Why would someone bring up love? Who talks about love? Is love a thing? He loved his mom.*)

DANA: My husband makes my lunch every night, and he makes it with love. We cook and clean together. We take turns on which show to watch. My two sons talk to me everyday. Yesterday when I came home from work my seventeen-year-old was asleep on the couch. Just lying there. You have that? Anyone sleeping on your couch?

RYAN: (*This interrogation is unbearable.*) I was thinking about getting a couple of cats.

DANA: Do you know anything? Like have you learned anything in life? You can't even hold a conversation with someone long enough to learn if they have kids or which country they grew up in. I do have compassion for you. I do. I don't have empathy though. I can't imagine what it would be like treating a twelve dolalr employee like a microbe.

RYAN: A microbe?

DANA: Yes, a microbe. I am going to go now. Good luck.

The next person that came in the office was Theo. Ryan had no idea how Theo felt about him. He was Bill's paralegal, not his. Ryan's paralegal was Yesenia, who had yet to come into the office and did not seem concerned with saying anything to him before he left forever.

THEO: We both have political science degrees, right?
RYAN: Yes, I have one.
THEO: I have a story to tell you. It resembles Jean-Jacques Rousseau's Discourse on Inequality. We are going to get French, European, Mediterranean in the Mojave Desert. We are far from Europe now, miles and time wise, but these Europeans can still haunt us, in a variety of ways. You aren't concerned though, you're white, yet you have never listened to Bach or Chopin or read John Austin or Dostoevsky, or even googled the paintings of Cezanne. You are what I would call "the new white person," a white person completely lacking any European anything, a total absence of European sensibility. You are American, a consumer, consuming products, and these products have names and prices, and you identify not with your authentic tastes, but you get your taste and sentiments from the taste factory. You love the taste factory. It requires no effort on your part to have authentic tastes, to create one's own aesthetic, because you are too busy for effort. A man like you has no time for effort. But to get back to my story. Let's take one hundred people and put them on an island with trees and an abundance of fruit and vegetables and some good soil. We have to remember, objectively, all one hundred people are completely equal in the beginning. They are just mammals or made in the image of God. You can pick one. It doesn't matter in this story. If someone is just an animal derived from evolution or made in the image of God, it makes them equal right? Catholics believe in both evolution and that we are created in the image of God, so Catholics really believe everyone is equal, regardless of how our bodies formed. Catholics actually believe that it is our capability to love that makes us like God, not our physical bodies.
RYAN: (*I'm Catholic, is that what they believe?*)

THEO: Now, we aren't going back to the Hobbes State of Nature that doesn't exist. Anthropology proves we were never that decrepit. We were always thinking, working, diligent creatures who could make things work in the face of catastrophic circumstances. Okay, so there are one hundred people. They are of the 2019 American mindset, but they don't even know it. They have no idea they are 2019 Americans. They just are. Use your imagination. These hundred people are going to build a civilization. So what is the thing that happens?

RYAN: They create a system of administration with democracy?

THEO: Oh man, you are fucking dumb. No. Ten of the most self-important people who are also competent, the ones really driven by self-centeredness and insecurity who demand that they always feel comfortable and secure, declare to the rest of them that they own everything, even the soil, even the trees, even the bushes, fuck, even the minerals and gasses that exist thousands of meters under the island. The entire island has been marked off into subdivisions, the land chosen based off of potable water and good soil. Seventy of them are too distracted trying to find people to marry and have families to notice that these ten people were busy marking off the island into grids. Then, the ten self-important people create courts and administrative bodies to handle the deeds of sale and more administrative bodies to handle taxes. Then, they offer minimal training to a random ten people from the seventy, to be trained in weaponry and violence. Then they announce that no one but the big ten can commit violence or theft. Everyone agrees this makes sense because they want to raise their families in a safe environment. Then the middle seventy realizes if they have no land to live on and no land to grow food, then how will they exist? That's a good question right? If I have no claim to any piece of land in a world where all the land is claimed, how do I exist?

RYAN: (*This pains me.*)

THEO: Well, the big ten notifies the middle seventy, if you farm our land and sell our goods to each other, then we will give you money, and you can give us the money and we will give you shelter on our land.

RYAN: If I am understanding, the big ten has convinced the middle seventy that they own no land because the big ten own all the land, therefore they should make things for the big ten, then the big ten will give them money, to buy things from the big ten, because the middle seventy has no things, because the big ten own all the capabilities to have and to make anything.

THEO: Yes, very good. The big ten has designed a civilization that feeds them like gods, it ensures that they reign like gods over the landscape, while the middle seventy thanks, even worships them for providing the opportunity to do their work. The middle seventy believe in the big ten like a religion. When the middle seventy person works forty hours a week but can't make rent, instead of blaming the big ten for inflating prices and lowering wages, they actually believe it is their own fault, and they hate themselves for their inability to gain more wealth. After many years of this, the middle seventy realized if they refused to do the big ten's work, then they could create situations where the big ten had to provide them with more money, but this didn't last long. The big ten felt annoyed by this. They invited workers from lesser developed islands to live on their island, to do the work that could only be done on their island, and then they sent work to lesser developed islands to do the work for cheaper on those islands. Then the big ten notified the middle seventy that the new workers were stealing their jobs, and that the workers on other islands were providing them with cheaper goods, so they didn't need to make more money because the goods had become so cheap. Some of the middle seventy got mad about the new workers on their island. The big ten did something truly great: they pretended there were two big fives, one five told the middle seventy that the new workers were bad, and the other five told them they were bringing diversity to the island. Then the middle seventy raged against each other, each one picking a side and fighting the other, thrusting themselves into terrible moods for the sake of their stance, which was provided to them to by the big ten, which was now two fives. The big ten noticed that this division was healthy for them. Every day they continued with an onslaught of hate for the other five. This was a winning strategy. No one even knew anymore that people owned things. Everyone in the middle seventy had become guilty and shameful to the point that they hated their own bodies. They were too busy ruminating about money and their own ugliness to notice reality anymore. Reality became chopped into even tinier realities until there were only small fragments of reality, and these realities were seen through the lenses of consumerist choices and the drug of self-righteousness. The middle seventy didn't even care about cosmology anymore. They didn't believe in God or that life on Earth was a momentary fluke. They didn't care anymore. The middle seventy had drifted into a dreamworld. (*Paused.*) I have a hard time describing the fundamentals of this new dreamworld. When I try, it comes off as an advertisement for a movie or a book, unrealistic. I think the thing is that the dreamworld the middle seventy is stuck in is so transitory and fragmented that there isn't really anything there, and this irrationality prompts them to proclaim ideological notions. It isn't that they sincerely believe in them, but they want others to know they endorse them. Even their non-endorsements become a form of endorsement.

RYAN: What about the twenty? You have left twenty people out.

THEO: They are the invisible, they are the disabled and psychologically confused.

RYAN: No one cares about them?

THEO: Not in this story.

RYAN: But I didn't do this, I didn't design this society. My talents have been a benefit to society.

THEO: Man, you are the empire of self-importance. You are the empire. It doesn't matter what talent landed you in the empire, it doesn't matter if you are an attractive pop singer or an astronomer or a lawyer and rise up by grit and talent alone, you believe in the design, and by believing it you become it. Christians become Christians by believing Jesus is the savior. You can't just call things by different names and hope they are different. You feel one hundred percent fine with walking past twelve-dollar employees and never questioning the oddness of your life.

RYAN: Who makes twelve dollars an hour?
THEO: The people who order the medical records.
RYAN: (*He had truly never thought about how much the medical records people make.*)
THEO: Ryan, you're a junkie and don't know it.
RYAN: I will consider what you have said today, thank you for supplying me with this information.

The last to come in was Tania (Ryan did not know her last name). Tania was a 32-year-old, five-foot tall woman who grew up in Tijuana and moved to San Diego in her teens. Her English was not excellent. If she was not at work, she did not speak English, and she barely spoke any language at work. Her job was to order medical records. Ordering medical records was the second to lowest job in a personal injury law firm. A medical records person sat at computer and sent letters requesting client's medical records. The letters were pre-made, so all they had to do was switch the client's name, put in their date of birth, the date of incident, and change the treater, as in, instead of it saying Radar Imaging, she would switch it to Red Rock Radiology. Tania did this all day. Sometimes she would call the medical treatment records department and ask for an update, but besides that her job was to put together a letter and then fax it, on repeat. She made 12 dollars an hour doing this. Tania was very nervous about her job. She wanted to do a good job, which led her to create reminder systems involving post-its and putting reminders to call people on the calendar. Inside Tania's little world, things were serious, her job gave her anxiety, she worried over the weekend if she had forgotten things. Sometimes she would be at home watching television with her boyfriend and suddenly remember she had forgotten to do something, and she would become worried. It would bother her all night. No one at the office knew she struggled so much.

Her work life was not nice though. The other medical request people didn't like her, they avoided her or straight-out condescended her to her face. Tania was tough, but she cried in her car after work.

Tania didn't want to get close to people. She didn't want to have to explain her life to anyone, to explain that she was a chiclet kid on the Tijuana border (When walking around Tijuana, especially in the 2000s, children would go up to tourists and ask them to buy chiclets) or that she grew up in different locations on the hills of Tijuana. She had seen and experienced things that the average white or Black or Latino American had never known. She did not want to speak of it. An American would get psychological help for such traumatic events, but Tania had little cultural reference for such a method. Additionally, she had no money for it. She had to live in the world no matter how bad her PTSD was. Her boyfriend Jorge was the same as she was, a chiclet kid from Mexico. When Tania went home at night, she was free from judgment, free from having to perform and live up to other people's standards. Jorge never condescended. He picked on her, which she loved, but he never condescended.

Tania would make breakfast every morning. Ham, sausage, eggs, peppers, onions, something different every morning. She would make herself lunch with leftovers from the dinner the night before. Tania ate lunch in her car, even though there was a kitchen for people to eat in, but she knew no one liked her, so she ate alone even when the temperature reached 107 degrees.

Tania never gossiped, and even though people did not treat her well, she never said, "They aren't worth it." Even though many people said that about her, she would say, "I think she just has a bad mood." The lawyers and office manager never knew everyone treated Tania badly. They never knew that she had so much anxiety regarding her job. If someone had told a lawyer, the lawyer would have thought, "My job is a thousand times harder than hers, what is she stressed about," not knowing or caring that the job was a bureaucratic nightmare and the stressful things about it had nothing to do with intelligence or diligence, but with absurd things like records departments not calling you back, or that the attorney won't speak to you because "I am too busy." Trying to keep every single medical record organized, making sure they all come on time. These tasks could at times become overly complicated and frustrating for anyone.

Ryan had a secret crush on Tania, and treated her with a different sense of kindness. The other medical request people noticed, and it made them torment Tania even more. The other medical request people gossiped that attorney Neroni had a crush on Tania, that Tania and Mr. Neroni were secretly having sex, that Mr. Neroni would help Tania attain a promotion to the pre-lit department. (Pre-lit, before litigation, a department that organizes medical records, does client intakes, organizes medical records, and sends Demand Letters to insurance companies. Paid a little more). Of course, this never happened. Ryan considered himself too busy to ever help someone's life get better.

Tania never noticed that Ryan had a crush on her. He would often ask about what she and her boyfriend did the previous weekend and what Tania cooked for breakfast. At no point, did the conversation become flirty, as in giggles or a passing shoulder touch. Underneath, Ryan would have died if Tania touched his shoulder. The excitement from Tania's hand would have made him feel like a schoolboy, and he desperately wanted to feel like a schoolboy again. Not all day. He didn't want to return to a state of adolescence. Just a nice ten minutes of new excitement would have made him happy.

He knew though, that as an attorney working at the most important law firm in Las Vegas, he could never date a medical request person. It would be like driving a used car. His career had rules. It was like a prison, but a prison that made you lots of money. He had to be prudent. He had to make decisions that directed the course of his life to a salvation, an earthly salvation, because he could have wonderful retirement years if he played his cards right.

TANIA: (*Speaking in Baja California Accent.*) Hello, Mr. Neroni.
RYAN: (*Looking at her face and body across from him caused a spontaneous sadness. He imagined her making him breakfast, sausage, peppers, and onions on a corn tortilla. Oh, it has to be wonderful to wake up with her in the morning, getting up early. First, she takes her shower and then you take yours. You take the garbage out, and she throws the onions in the skillet. You set the table, and she stirs the eggs. Then you go to work, text her on your break, she writes back something nice, the day ends, you drive home knowing that Tania will be there, and she will tell you things and you will tell her things, you will poke fun at each other, then you go to bed. Decades pass, then you have this*

TANIA: I wanted to say it was nice working with you.

RYAN: Really?

TANIA: Yes, you always responded to my emails, and told me good job.

RYAN: I was always happy with your work.

TANIA: (*She smiled.*)

RYAN: I'm going to leave today. Would you like my mouse or mouse pad?
I also have a very nice gel butt pad if you like.

TANIA: Oh, that sounds nice. I've always wanted a butt pad, my chair,
you know, it's hard.

RYAN: Okay, before I leave, I'll drop them off at your desk.

TANIA: Oh, thank you, Mr. Neroni.

Chapter 5

Ryan was sitting on the couch with his mom. His mom was relaxing by watching a show about a serial killer who murdered two women and used a lot of bleach to destroy DNA. His mother loved these shows.

RYAN: Mom. I quit my job today.
MARGARET: Oh good.
RYAN: (*This was not the response Ryan expected. She had always encouraged him to become a lawyer. She had even paid for his LSAT prep class and had sent him a monthly allowance when he lived in Chicago. She had also sent him a box full of shampoos, soaps, razors, shirts, underwear and pants every two months. She visited him once every semester for a weekend to make sure he was doing all right. He remembered those days fondly, walking around with his mom, showing her things in the city. He liked to show his mom things. But "Oh good." What did that mean? He felt a surge of anger, almost. Was she betraying him? Had she betrayed him? How long had she been thinking that his life was not going well? But to respond with that line of inquisition would be ungrateful. He chose not to do that, but to continue talking about himself.*) My accountant told me that I would have around twelve thousand dollars deposited monthly into my bank account for the next thirty years. I, hmm, (*pause*), I couldn't pull it off anymore. I mean, I win right? I have enough money to live the rest of my life. I just can't justify working nine to twelve hours a day for decades when I already have more money than most of humanity. I mean, I don't know what the "what" is anymore, like, you know, who what where why when. I have lost the "what" and the "why" when it comes to being an attorney. It feels like I woke up a different person. When I look

back on my life, maybe I wasn't smart at all. All my life I've been convinced I was smart, that I was competent, that I had everything under control, that I was a serious person, but no one remembers me. I don't even have any real friends. Everyone I talk to is part of that world. It wasn't like we made friends but built a safety net. I feel like I have lost faith, like I have lost my religion.

MARGARET: Well, things were easy for you. You are competent, you had college-educated parents, you grew up with a predictable set of positive and negative reinforcement feedback. You never experienced excessive violence, so you have zero PTSD. Most people have some PTSD. I hate to say it, but most people have some level of brain damage. Most people have had a harder life than you.

RYAN: (*He did not dispute that.*) I don't understand why though or what for? There is no logic to the distribution of irrational hardship.

MARGARET: (*She looked at her boy. He looked sad. She never liked to see him sad, but it looked like this sadness might be good for him. She could see for a while that a sadness was overtaking him. The boy didn't understand why he worked so hard to come home and sleep alone. He didn't understand why he had to do so many things not related to being a lawyer at all to be a lawyer: the fancy car, loving the Golden Knights, having a maid, talking about how Defense lawyers were pieces of shit, organizing an underpaid staff, constantly learning new editions of Adobe, law-office management software, Microsoft Word, PowerPoint, Excel, answering emails, learning new case law, getting constant haircuts, gelling his hair every morning, living this busy version of life. And for what? Ryan could no longer come up with reasonable answers to be himself.*) What will you do now?

RYAN: I'm going to learn how to be a person. I have to learn about people that are not like me. I think though—I read an article—and it said in order to lose self-importance, one must help those who do not give thanks. It is like a practice. You just don't read something, take a test and become a person. No one is ever going to test if you became a person or not. You have to do it. You have to test yourself. You have to practice and motivate yourself. There is no money in becoming a person, so no one sells it. But what I would really like to do is, I want to be a bootlegger.

MARGARET: A bootlegger? Like Burt Reynolds or the Dukes of Hazzard.

RYAN: Yeah, like that.

MARGARET: Seems funny. (*Laughter.*)

Chapter 6

Written on a post-it: Personal Goal of the Day: Say something nice to a woman I am not sexualy attracted to, and compliment a man.

It was the first day of Ryan's freedom. He slept late, until 8:30 a.m. He took a shower. He didn't know how to feel yet. His feelings were still with work, still thinking about work, still thinking about everyone he knew at work, the work, and all the things about work that bothered him.

After his shower, he stood naked in front of the mirror. He reached down to grab the hair gel like an automaton, like a droid with only one programming. His hand stopped before it reached the gel. He looked at the gel. He grabbed the gel and threw it in the garbage. He would never apply gel to his hair again. He would not get haircuts every ten days, but every other month like a normal person. He wouldn't even really comb his hair anymore. He put on his cheapest looking clothes, chinos and a navy blue t-shirt. He looked in the mirror again. He didn't look like anything, just another invisible person.

Ryan's first stop was at the Tesla store. He went in the building.

RYAN: I don't want this car anymore, please take it back.
TESLA PERSON: Really?
RYAN: Please.

It was a complicated process full of signing papers, waiting and waiting some more, but he was used to waiting and signing papers. It was not a frustrating process. With the Tesla gone, he had to order an Uber.

The Uber driver was an old white man who started talking about how his wife died six years previously. He had enough money to live, but he felt bored and wanted to talk to people, which led him to driving for Uber.

RYAN: (*No one ever spoke to me like this when I was in a suit with my hair gelled. What is happening? Is this human affection?*) Are you from here?

UBER DRIVER: No, I'm from Houston, but I've always loved Vegas, so my wife and I decided to move here in 2003. It was great in 2003, endless jobs, everything was growing. When 2008 came, it really threw us for a loop.

RYAN: (*Ryan remembered 2008. Bad years followed in Las Vegas. The recession never affected his life, not for one day.*) Did the recession cause you to lose your job? What happened?

UBER DRIVER: I lost some of my retirement. My wife lost her job at the casino. It altered our end of life forecast, I guess. Then she got cancer, in the lungs, she loved cigarettes, and instead of living till our eighties together I am spending these last years alone.

RYAN: (*I am spending my whole life alone. He misses her. It seems very real to him.*) How did you meet her?

UBER DRIVER: We met in high school, we pretty much always knew each other, but never really spoke, but then in eleventh grade we started talking. We were both really young then. (*He says "really young" like it is a location, a vacation somebody once took that blew their mind and even changed them a little bit, but they will never return to that location again for the rest of their lives.*) We got married one year out of high school. We had three kids together. One of them even lives in Las Vegas. I babysit my granddaughter at least twice a week.

The man kept going and going, sadness and happiness, ups and downs, all the twists and turns of a man's life. Ryan sat in the back seat, only half caring. The driver's narrative was a bit obvious and heavy-handed, he thought.

The Uber Driver dropped him off at the Honda dealership. He said goodbye to the old man and his dead wife.

He wanted two cars, a cheap car and a Honda Civic Type R. He went into the dealership and asked for help. They told him to sit down and wait. He looked around and saw a middle-aged Hispanic woman, a woman he was not in anyway sexually attracted to, with her teenage daughter. The woman had cool hair, thought. It looks really nice, Ryan thought. He looked at her.

RYAN: Ma'am, you have really great hair.
WOMAN: Thank you. (*She smiled.*)

The car dealer finally came for Ryan. He was a young handsome African-American man, tall and slender. Age had not caught up with his belly. He had a warm smile. They sat at a desk in a glass cubicle. The dealer immediately tried to find common ground by mentioning the Golden Knights. This was enough. Ryan was able to say he had seen some games previously. He did not mention he once had season tickets.

CAR DEALER: For our paperwork, we require your occupation and income.
RYAN: (*Wrote down unemployed and income of $150,550.04.*)
CAR DEALER: (*Looked down at income number, looked up at Ryan.*) Your income is quite high but you have no job?
RYAN: No, I am unemployed.
CAR DEALER: Okay. We also require a credit check.
RYAN: That's fine.
The car dealer went and did a credit check. He came back.
CAR DEALER: Your credit is perfect. What car would you like to look at first?
RYAN: I want an all black—I mean all black, even the rims, tinted windows—2019 Honda Civic Type R standard. I also want a specific option. If I need to go to another dealership, please tell me. It is okay.
CAR DEALER: Okay, what is it?
RYAN: I would like the brake lights to have an option where I click a switch, and if I brake they don't turn on. I mean, I want working brake lights, of course, but I want to be able to click (made hand motion for clicking) and turn off the brake lights.

CAR DEALER: (*This dude is doing criminal shit, damn*) Well sir, we here at Peterson's Honda Dealership can paint your car completely black and install tinted windows, but as for black rims and a switch to turn off brake lights, let me go check with my mechanics.

The car dealer left. Ryan played on his phone. He felt carefree, peaceful for the first time in years. The car dealer returned.

CAR DEALER: Okay, one of our mechanics. His name is Roberto. (*He slid a piece of paper with a name and number on it across the desk to Ryan. Ryan put it in his pocket.*) Roberto is our best man. He has his own drag car and races it regularly. He gets cars from junkyards and rebuilds them from scratch. I'm sure Roberto can do it or at least direct you to the right person.

RYAN: Thank you. I appreciate your assistance. Now, I want another car.

CAR DEALER: Two cars. Great. What else would you like?

RYAN: Do you have like a grandma car, like a car that a grandma drove and is like fifteen years old?

CAR DEALER: Yes we do. We just got a 2003 Toyota Corolla with only eighty-two thousand miles. A grandpa, not a grandma, drove it, but they parked it in the garage the entire time, and it runs like new.

RYAN: I'll take it right now.

CAR DEALER: You don't want to drive it?

RYAN I want to be surprised.

For the next two hours Ryan Neroni filled out paperwork, writing his name over and over again. The car dealer eventually told him he had a wonderful wife, and that he was in the Air Force and that's how he ended up in Las Vegas. Ryan never mentioned that he had been an attorney or that he had just won the biggest case in Las Vegas history. He told him that he lived with his mom and was thinking about visiting the Bonneville Salt Flats.

The next stop for Ryan was lunch. Driving the 2003 Toyota Corolla was hard to get used to after driving a Tesla. It reminded him of the 1999 Chevy Cavalier he drove in Chicago during law school, a slow easy-to-drive vehicle that served no other purpose but to get people to work.

He never went to cheap Chinese places, but times were different. He walked in and a Chinese woman motioned for him to sit at a specific table. He looked around the Chinese place. The customers were Hispanic, African-American, and white. No one had suits on. There was a group of men wearing construction outfits.

A young Chinese woman came to the table. Ryan ordered orange chicken lunch.

RYAN: (*These are non-model minority Asians, no doctors or professors here. Who were these people? What was their passage from China to Las Vegas like? What do they do after work? How do they live in a world where they knew little of the dominant language? He had never thought about these people before. They were always there, living and working right beside him, but not once his entire life had he considered them relevant, as part of his community.*)

When Ryan was in line to pay, a white couple, an overweight man with a beard that had not been trimmed in months and a woman that looked burnt and malnourished, started yelling at the cashier that their food was horrible and they demanded a full refund. The cashier explained they did not give full refunds but would be happy to remake their food. Ryan watched this whole event take place. The woman kept yelling, completely convinced that she had the right to a free meal. Ryan compared the rights of a free meal to the Bill of Rights in his head:

RYAN: (*The right of the people to be against unreasonable food, shall not be violated, and ye shall have the full bill refunded if the meal improperly served.*)

Then the overweight man threw the food into the air. It landed on a nearby seat, the rice going everywhere. Ryan stared at the scattered rice, feeling bad for the non-model minority Asians.

RYAN: (*To the server.*) Look that man is throwing food.

The young woman looked at the scattered rice and the angry man and just stood there frozen.

Ryan paid his bill. When he was walking out the angry lady yelled at him.

ANGRY WHITE LADY: Thanks for being self-serving. Go back to the garbage can where you live.

Ryan laughed and walked back to his car.

RYAN: (*Sitting in his car, holding the steering wheel.*) I live in a fucking garbage can. Doesn't self-serve mean like self-serve gas or self-serving soda machine. (*He was deeply confused by this incident. Is this normal at Chinese places? Do non-model minority Asians have to deal with this every day? Is food service really a constitutional right? During trials he would often make the argument to the jury that never getting rear-ended and never slipping on grapes was a constitutional right.*)

Next stop Smith's grocery store. Usually Ryan never went to Smith's. It was cheap and the cheapest people went there. He went to Sprouts and Wholefoods. Today was a new day though. He was going to Smith's.

Ryan parked his car in the Smith's parking lot. He got out of the car and looked around. There was a swap meet called Rainbow Plaza Mall, a Great Cuts, a pawn store, a Burger King, a used bookstore, a taco truck and a Smith's. He wanted to know what was inside the swap meet. He had never been to one his entire life.

RYAN: (*Holy shit what is this place?*)

There was a section operated by an African-American woman that sold weaves, netcaps, sweaters, jeans, and work clothes. As he walked around looking at the clothes, it occurred to him they were the clothes of poor people he saw. He recalled several of the office workers wearing clothes like these on casual Friday. He decided to buy some shirts.

In another section there was a Korean lady sewing football jerseys.

[44]

She was making clothes inside of the store. Then he noticed there were Koreans and African-Americans everywhere. Never in his life did he know there was a place of commerce that African-Americans and Koreans shared. Then he found a section run by a Mexican woman, with very complicated hair and make-up. She was selling CDs of banda music and belts with large belt buckles and various other things that Ryan did not understand.

Eventually he found a section where a Korean lady sold toys for children. He stood in front of the toys wondering about the kids who might play with the toys.

Ryan left the swap meet and went to Smith's. In the parking lot a 20-something white man yelled from 15 feet away. He had an unkept beard and was wearing no shirt.

SHIRTLESS MAN: Hey, you think this is bullshit right?
RYAN: What is bullshit?
SHIRTLESS MAN: Man, you don't know shit.
RYAN: (*Is this a real conversation?*)

The shirtless man kept walking.
The inside of Smith's was overwhelming to Ryan. He looked at the diverse body types and lack of concern for fashion and felt awkward. No one seemed concerned with having shame. He overheard an old white man talking to the young white man at the deli.

OLD WHITE MAN: Obama didn't do anything, he didn't do a damn thing, that's how we got into this mess, nothing was done.

The deli person did not nod or give any sort of facial expression that implied he was even listening.

OLD WHITE MAN: (*To Ryan.*) Don't you agree? He didn't do anything and that's how we got into this mess?
RYAN: (*In his previous life, he would have told the old white man that he did know what he was talking about, and to please stop talking.*) Sir, I apol-

ogize. I have never voted in my life, nor do I have any interest in politics.

OLD WHITE MAN: (*Confused by the long compound sentence, frightened.*) Well, I understand that.

Ryan moved to the fruit section and heard an African-American mother say to her five-year-old child.

MOM: You want what?

CHILD: Raspberries.

MOM: I just fucking got you fucking peaches. Now you want fucking rasperberries? Shut the fuck up.

The child looked sad.

When Ryan entered the parking lot, there was a ruckus happening. The shirtless man had picked a fight with a 40-something Mexican man. The Mexican man was in a boxing pose. The Mexican man showed no fear.

SHIRTLESS MAN: I'm going to fuck you up. You're a piece of shit, man. You love this bullshit, man. All the bullshit you love.

The Mexican man did not understand this diatribe. The Mexican man moved closer. The shirtless man yelled.

SHIRTLESS MAN: Oh you want to fight now!

The security guard, a 60-something white woman, was watching from 20 feet away. She wasn't even on the phone with the cops. She was smoking a cigarette.

SECURITY GUARD: (*To a Filipino woman selling bracelets in the parking lot.*) These boys are gonna fight.

A teenager was recording the event for their Instagram.

[46]

The Mexican man threw a jab, then a right, connecting with the shirtless man's chin. The shirtless man attempted a punch, but the Mexican man immediately went out of range. The shirtless man backed up ten feet and continued yelling at a distance.

Ryan went to his car and drove to the gas station. When he arrived at the gas station, he saw a young Black man with a 1984 Camaro painted black and red.

RYAN: That's a cool car.
YOUNG MAN: Thanks.

An older African-American man walked up to Ryan.

RYAN: (*This man looks homeless, he has all the signifiers of hoboness.*)
HOMELESS MAN: Sir, may I have five dollars?
RYAN: Yes, let me go in and get cash back, and I'll give it to you. Do you need water?
HOMELESS MAN: Yes, thanks.

Ryan went into the store, bought several bottled waters and got a 20 dollar bill to give to the man.

After he went outside he could no longer find the man. The man had disappeared. He stood there holding two large bottled waters and a 20 dollar bill.

Chapter 7

Ryan and Margaret entered the church for 10 a.m. mass. They shook hands at the door with the liturgical ministers, crossed themselves with holy water, walked down to their preferred row, genuflected, and took a seat.

Mass went as usual. First came the three readings, songs, and then the priest provided a homily. Going to mass was an honorable duty he held towards his mother. It was a duty he held towards all of Italy and their long history with the church. For the longest time though, it was a duty to have a religion with other lawyers. The other lawyers all had a religion, either Jewish or Mormon or some version of Christian. He didn't want to be the one without religion. They might find it offensive. But what was the purpose now that he had left? He had become as invisible as everyone else. What point did having a religion serve?

PRIEST: (*An old Jesuit, retired, only giving mass when the main priests were on vacation or attending to other duties. The old Jesuit didn't mind, he loved giving mass. Unlike Ryan, he stayed committed and in love with his chosen profession.*) (*He walked from behind the ambo and stood in front of everyone and spoke. He had a headset microphone, his hands were free.*) For all of human history—and I do not just mean white history, but peoples living on all continents—when they found out the foundation of their metaphysics, it usually came in the form of a story. For us it is Moses and Jesus, for others Buddha or Lao Tzu, and the indigenous peoples of the Americas, they have their own stories, and Africans have their own stories, the stories combined metaphysics, ethics, and rituals that guided people through life. Humanity obviously prefers these three aspects of human existence to be located in the same building in town. They obviously prefer that there is some sort of metaphysics, that the metaphysics implies an ethics, and that these institutions organize rituals that guide people through the different stages of life. Now, I know in different cultures these rituals can be vastly different, but still, there is something in the human DNA that enjoys rituals. After the Renaissance, things changed. Metaphysics became physics, ethics found itself in political science departments, and rituals were the only things churches had left to rule over. God became math problems. Ethics became four hundred-page books that most people could never understand and had no music. There was no great story to their books, nothing to reinforce in the human heart that ethics were important. Where does that leave us now? Five hundred years later, there are more people than ever, and each one feels lost. They feel and logically can piece together that the system they live in is irrational. To tolerate this irrationality, this lack of unity, they do drugs, they consume themselves with entertainment, they dream of one day being rich and having a personal heaven on Earth, they become obsessed with their careers, they do everything they can to avoid the feeling that this might all be irrational. I'm not saying science is bad. I'm not saying religion can't be blamed for this schism in the human spirit. I'm saying that humanity craves that metaphysics, ethics, and ritual be in the same building. We have taken the same view as our governments, checks and balances, by separating metaphysics, ethics and ritual. We have defused the power of each institution. Metaphysics is located on college campuses and one can only know the secrets of physics if one has a very high IQ and has the ability to do math at incredible levels. One of the funniest things I always see in movies is when the Catholic Church gets accused of "holding secrets." What do any of us know about physics? I bet there isn't one physicist here. (*There were none.*) What do any of us know about ethics? Has anyone read John Rawls or Kant? Contemporary ethics destroyed all of religion, the Ancient Greeks, and all of Chinese philosophy with a question regarding a trolley. (*Ryan remembered the day he spent talking about the trolley at college. He remembered being confused by it.*) (*Most of the people in the pews were completely confused by what was happening.*) What about ritual? The milestones of life? For most people, they are all gone. Rituals notify the individual that they have new responsibilities, their life has changed, they must commit themselves to a new course, there is no turning back. Now, imagine, if you were not capable of finding yourself a career in physics, not capable of understanding books of ethics, and completely without rituals, and you didn't even know that you were completely lost, you didn't know anything about the universe you found yourself in, you didn't know how to behave, and you didn't know that each stage of life contained new and different responsibilities. What would happen to that person? They would either remain confused or choose a set of lies. Those are our choices in this world, confusion or lies. Confusion leads to a stumbling life, and lies lead you to success. People have been saying for centuries that the Church is a lie, that if one leads a healthy life of forgiveness, one can go to heaven after one dies. But they have replaced it with the idea that if one deadens their sense of ethics and consumes themselves with self-importance, ignores the suffering of the world, forgets everything that gives life meaning, then you too can become rich and have a stock portfolio. We will take away the sin of sex, as long as you believe in the accumulation of capital at the expense of others. I'm not saying sex is bad. I'm not saying that at all. It is an odd trade-off though, and no one noticed they made it. Everyone, and I mean everyone, is standing there screaming, "This is all I have! This is all I have!" because we no longer have anything. Previously, we all shared the same God. We shared similar institutions. We shared things and believed in this sharing, and through sharing we had big things, together. Now, we share nothing. I'm not even sure Catholics share the same God anymore. I'm not crying nostalgia. I see that a new world is coming, a world of less racism, sexism, sexuality and xenophobia. I know it is ending because a subdivision of the world is fighting desperately to conserve previous notions about how humans should live. I can hear them screaming, "This is all I have! This is all I have!" A new world is rising out of the ashes of the Renaissance. I don't know if it will be a horrifying world. It might be a horrifying a world to me and my sentiments, but it might be a great world. (*The Priest often wondered if his whole life was a dream, if he had lived in a transitory cultural dreamland that died as soon as it was born. This thought gave him peace. It allowed for him to forgive.*) Sadly, we are all living at the end of one world and the beginning of a new one. The Renaissance's winter is over. The snows have melted and the streams have flooded to make new canyons. Where does Jesus fit into all this? What can we cling to in this complex confusion that never supplies us with a concrete reality, so we can stop feeling like we are trapped in an Escher painting? I think we can all relate to this event in life. Most of us have experienced it, or we have at least seen it many times. Have you ever seen a three-year-old open their arms, and their mom or dad bend over and pick them up and hold them tightly to their chest. The child's little arms wrap around the parent. We have to stop for a minute and try to understand what a three-year-old is. It is helpless. It cannot survive without help. It screams out for assistance in every small task in life. But what else, what we do not speak of, is that no one knows how the three-year-old will turn out. This child could grow up and be a selfish drug addict or a violent spouse abuser, a person that abandons their children. They could grow up to be a terrible person, yet the parent picks them up. The child has complete faith in the parent, and the parent contains enough love to carry the child. And what about the parent? They could be a drug addict, violent, selfish, they could be a terrible person, intent if they know it or not on raising a useless person. And yet, the child still believes. The child doesn't know that in eighteen years they are going to tell that parent to screw off and never speak to them again. That they will move two thousand miles to another city and only see their parents on holidays. The child does not know who their parents really are, and the parent does not know who the child will become, but at that moment both people trust completely that this is the right thing to do. Forgiveness starts with your ability to oscillate between these two modes of being, between being helpless and carrying those that need help, regardless of the outcome.

Chapter 8

Ryan was done with work for a week. He was lying on his couch trying to read a book. He hadn't read a book for 100% enjoyment in years. He couldn't relax, though. His body ached. It hurt in a way like it was cramping up, which made his mind cramp. He felt compelled to touch someone, to be close to anyone. He didn't understand this urge. Why was his body notifying him it was time to touch and be touched? He had hoped this impulse would have gone away by now. He had this urge since he was a teenager, same as everyone else. He couldn't understand why he couldn't rise above it, grow out of it. Sexuality for Ryan was never natural. He was picky and took too much pride in it. That was his problem. Everything became an issue of doing it well, which led him to be selfish and annoying. He was an annoying person. He knew that. He was an annoying lover, and, more than anything, he was controlling. When things didn't go his way, a surge of bad energy shot into his body. To defeat this bad feeling, he asserted more control over the people around him. Obviously it was impossible to completely surround himself with people who could be controlled, therefore he reduced the amount of people he was around, until there was only his mother.

Going on a dating website seemed like it would create a situation where he had no control. He would go to the date, and who knows what would happen. The uncertainty of the event was catastrophic to him. If she was insane, who knows how he would have to behave to get through the date, and then he would have to notify her via text message that he didn't like her, and he would have to hurt her. If she didn't like him, he would be the one hurt. There was a chance she might like him, then they might kiss, and she would tell him that his breath smelled horrible.

Women were too dangerous for Ryan. It wasn't that Ryan did not like women. He believed in feminism. He'd helped multiple women attorneys and legal staff get hired at his firm and at other firms. There was no record of him trying to groom or have sex with any of the young interns in his career. One time, in his early 20s, he felt angry at a girl for not having sex with him, and she asked him to sleep on the couch. He laid down on her couch and went to sleep. Something else was wrong. It was like his mind couldn't take a leap anymore. Ryan often looked at other couples and wondered how they pulled it off. Ryan couldn't fathom how so many deranged and homely people had sex with each other and made babies. He knew it was a ridiculous narcissistic vain thought, but he had it. There was an attorney at his law firm named Peterson. He was 100 pounds overweight, his skin a pale sickly white, big hands that looked like chewed gum. He was lazy, rude and excessively self-important, and yet he had been married for 22 years. He had two kids. He couldn't imagine someone being sexually aroused enough to have sex with Peterson. These weren't thoughts of jealousy, but a desperate want for coherence in the world.

Ryan also wanted to touch a penis. He had never had this feeling in his life until recently. He was masturbating to internet porn and saw a penis and thought, "Wow, that looks nice. I want to grab it." The feeling seemed ridiculous to him. First he wanted to finger vaginas and now he wants to cuddle a penis in his hand. What next? He actually laughed at himself. He watched some gay porn but chest hair seemed gross to him. He also didn't like how men did their hair. He liked makeup. He tried watching transgender porn and it fit nicely. He could have never predicted this was going to be a thing in his life, yet it was. He didn't like objectifying the people in porn, but he didn't know what to do. He couldn't pull anything else off, and he needed to ejaculate because rubbing one's genitals and orgasms are calming.

RYAN: This is the day I do something about this feeling. (*He was terrified. His entire life was directed at being a judge or the head partner of a large law firm. He had remained clean for his entire life for goals that no longer existed. Now, he had no goals.*)

He downloaded Grindr on his phone and began looking at pictures of transgender women. He messaged several of them and received no response. He messaged them again and still did not receive a response. He decided to write "$160?"

A woman named Patta responded.

PATTA: Hi how are you
RYAN: I'm doing well. How are you
PATTA: Good. I give massage, do you want massage
RYAN: Yes, that sounds nice.
PATTA: Okay. $160 is good
RYAN: Yes
PATTA: I live by Palms, park at Chevron.
RYAN: Okay
PATTA: When will you be here
RYAN: Thirty minutes
PATTA: Okay I get ready

His heart started racing. He felt excited, like truly excited. He never understood this excitement that would arise in him regarding sexuality. It was the most normal thing in the world for most people, but for Ryan it felt like a panic attack. Previously he didn't like these feelings. They felt like losing control, but now he was ready to indulge.

He drove through Las Vegas. It was mid-November and the temperature and sun were okay. It was nice to drive with the window down. He randomly wondered if Patta might be a police officer and this was just an elaborate sting operation, that he would get arrested for said criminal activity and have his face in the Las Vegas Review Journal, and his mom would feel sad because she had raised a man who did said criminal activity.

He arrived at the address Patta provided, it looked like a normal boring house. It wasn't a nice house, just a house.

His heart was beating rapidly.

Ryan imagined the door opening and the police being there, arresting him, being in a police car, being overwhelmed with emotions that he would prefer not to have. Then he settled into it, it would be funny, the University of Chicago attorney becomes a john. It would show that he had truly lost his mind and become some sort of rebel. Actually, he realized, this was Las Vegas. Everyone probably did this. If a lot of people didn't do this, these services wouldn't be easily accessible. You couldn't have a business without customers.

Ryan knocked on the door. He waited there, panicking. Patta cracked the door and looked at him.

PATTA: Okay, come.
RYAN: Hi.
PATTA: Hi. Take your shoes off.

Ryan removed his shoes.
He looked around the house, a couch, a flat screen television, pictures on the walls. A kitchen table, microwave, sink, stove. It all looked excessively normal. He'd been hoping for maybe something more creepy. There wasn't one creepy thing about this house.

PATTA: Follow me.

Ryan followed into her bedroom. There was one lamp on, the bulb low wattage. There was a massage table. There was a comfortable looking bed and another flat screen television and a laptop on the bed. A complete lack of creepiness.

RYAN: (*This is nothing like it is in the movies.*)
PATTA: Clothes. (*Hand motion indicating disrobe.*)

Ryan removed his clothes and put them on the bed. He took the money out of his wallet.

RYAN: Where should I put the money?

She pointed to the dresser on which the flat-screen television sat. Ryan set the money on the dresser.

He sat on the massage table. Patta stood there wearing a robe. She untied the robe and took it off, revealing a complicated lingerie work uniform. She motioned for him to lay on his stomach.

For about ten minutes she massaged his back. She applied lotion, and it was not professional. Her skill set was nominal, but Ryan didn't care.

After 15 minutes had passed, she flipped him over, applied lotion and lightly caressed his chest, legs, and genitals for several minutes.

Ryan was looking at her. She smiled. She pushed her underwear over and revealed a small uncircumsized penis. Ryan looked at it and felt a rush of excitement go through his body. He felt happy, the sexy happy, the happiness that overrides one's systems of judgment and rationality and was sadly too fleeting.

He reached out and felt it in his hands. He liked it. It was warm and grew underneath his fingers. He liked the sheath, how it ended, covering the penis. Ryan was circumcised and had never encountered an uncircumcised penis. He found it fascinating on a medical level. He wanted to study it, but he knew that was weird. He maintained the course of trying to have an orgasm.

Patta retrieved a different type of lubricant and applied it to her hand, and then to his hand. She jerked him off while he did the same for her (He really wasn't doing it for her; he was doing it for him.) It did not take long. He came on his stomach. Patta smiled.

PATTA: Okay.
RYAN: Wow.

Patta handed him a box of tissues. She sat on the bed.

RYAN: Do you work?
PATTA: Yes, at a Thai restaurant. But things are not good. I am only
getting three days a week. I used to get five days a week, but the
place I worked, it closed. I had to get a new job, and they only give

me three days a week.

RYAN: That sounds terrible.

PATTA: What do you do?

RYAN: I don't do anything anymore. I have no job.

PATTA: (*She looked confused.*) How long have you lived here?

RYAN: All my life. I lived in Chicago for a little.

PATTA: Chicago, in the east?

RYAN: Yes.

PATTA: I've never been east.

RYAN: How long have you been here?

PATTA: Four years. I was married, but not anymore. Are you married?

RYAN: No. Are most men that get massages married?

PATTA: Yes.

RYAN: (*Trying to think of things to say while he dressed. He didn't want silence.*) Do you live with family?

PATTA: No, I have a roommate. She worked with me at the restaurant where I worked five days a week.

RYAN: Okay, got it. I live with my mom.

PATTA: That must be nice. I wished I lived with my mom.

Ryan finished dressing. Patta put her robe back on and walked him through the house. There was a room they passed through that had several Buddhist statues and floor mats. Ryan stopped and looked at the room.

RYAN: You are Buddhist?

PATTA: Yes.

RYAN: Do you mediate, attend a temple?

PATTA: Yes, I meditate in the morning. There is a temple on Gowan Street, I go there.

RYAN: (*A Buddhist? This isn't turning out to be creepy at all. This verges on wholesome.*)

PATTA: (*While both were looking at the Buddhist statues, Patta put her hand on Ryan's shoulder. He looked down at her.*) You will have a mission soon.

RYAN: (*A mission? That sounds nice. I have never been on a mission or a vision quest or a journey, more like, my life has been a series of events that demanded I conform to protocol.*) I like that.

She walked him to the door and opened it. Ryan walked though.

PATTA: Bye.
RYAN: Bye.

Chapter 9

Ryan went to Starbucks on Lake Mead and Buffalo in the hope of feeling like a person by being around people. Never in his life had he sat around and done nothing inside a coffee shop.

He stepped out of his car and was immediately confronted by a homeless person. He was an old white man with a shaggy beard, dirt covered clothes, and eyes that couldn't focus. Ryan stared at him.

RYAN: (*This is a homeless person. A person without shelter. A person that is so friendless, not one human with shelter would give him a room or couch to sleep. Maybe he doesn't know what is happening. His brain no longer works. Amazing that his motor skills and habits to attain food remain intact. This man has lived to an old age. He didn't even go to the University of Chicago to live to an old age. I wonder what happened to his brain that it no longer works. I need to have empathy. I'm sleeping outside, no one loves me. All the things I've done in my life led to me sleeping outside. Maybe I am too nuts to think normal thoughts. I sleep on the ground having scattered thoughts about who knows what.*)

HOMELESS MAN: May I have a dollar?

RYAN: (*This is all this man wants, one dollar. What a bargain.*) (*Ryan did not speak. He handed him 20 dollars, then walked away quickly.*)

HOMELESS MAN: God bless.

Before Ryan entered the Starbucks he saw a man in his 40s, dressed in a skintight spandex bicycle outfit, standing next to a bicycle. The man was leaning back on a column, arching his back a little, wearing sunglasses. Ryan considered it a strange pose for a man to take, then he noticed that the shape of the man's penis was visible through his spandex shorts. His penis was right there. He was a shower, approximately four and a half inches. If hard, there would be definite girth. Ryan looked at the penis, definitely circumsized, wondering if he should flick it. He decided not to do that.

Ryan purchased iced coffee and sat at a table. He took out a laptop. He did not know what he would do with his laptop. He did not have Facebook or Twitter or Instagram. He had zero social media. Today he was going to open a Facebook account. He was going to look at his extended family's lives and the lives of people he went to highschool with and his exes. He wanted to creep on everyone's pages and do calculations to figure out why his life had turned out comical.

Before he could start his Facebook page, a young Hispanic woman, Mayan looking (actually Zapotec), dressed in business casual, estimated age of 26, stood in front of him.

YOUNG WOMAN: May I sit down?
RYAN: (*She is pretty. Is this what normal people do? Sit with strangers?*) Yes, of course. (*He closed his laptop and became an avid listener.*)
THERESA: My name is Theresa Barahona, what's yours?
RYAN: Ryan.
THERESA: Are you having a nice day?
RYAN: Yes, it is great.
THERESA: What job do you do Ryan?
RYAN: I have no job.
THERESA: No job. Are you in between jobs?
RYAN: I don't have one.
THERESA: You're the kind of person that wants to escape the rat race aren't you?
RYAN: Yes, of course. (*She is reading my mind.*)
THERESA: I want to escape the race rat too. I just couldn't see the point of working for decades for other people, being controlled by other people, getting up day after day, being told what to do. See, I worked at a casino in retail. I couldn't see myself working in retail my whole life. I don't want to live a humdrum life, Ryan. I want to live an ex-

citing life. I want to travel the world.

RYAN: (*A deep sense of confusion about where this was going, but his face remained avid and concerned.*)

THERESA: Luckily I met my life coach, my mentor. My mentor has taught me about stocks and bonds, Roth IRAs, hedge funds, and a million ways a person can make money without doing any work.

RYAN: (*This is the same premise statement a communist had in the 20th century, but turned upside. Wow, where is this going?*)

THERESA: My mentor has taught me many things. He has taught me what clothes to wear, how to do my hair, and what I need to do to succeed without doing any work. He is training me to become a Life Coach. My mentor has helped me identify my passions and priorities, which led to him helping me to develop an Action Plan.

RYAN: An Action Plan?

THERESA: Yes, an Action Plan. The mentor sits with me and asks me questions to help me think deeply about what I want out of life. Then he helped me create a plan that would help me attain my goals. He has also told me to read books such as *Think and Grow Rich*, *Positive Thinking Power*, *Big Money*, *Rich Dad Poor Dad*, *Success at all Costs*, *Money Money Money*, *Goals that Lead to Big Money*, *Thinking Money Thinking Big*, *The Secret*, and *How to be a Leader to get Rich*. My mentor says that after I read all those books I will be a changed person; I will have reached Money Enlightenment. Ryan, do you want to reach Money Enlightenment?

RYAN: (*I don't want her to leave the table. I am lonely.*) Yes.

THERESA: That makes me so happy for you, Ryan. I promise this is the best choice of your life. You will always look back on this moment with fondness, the day you decided to reach Money Enlightenment. You are on your way to traveling the world and escaping the rat race. You won't have to care about looking for jobs anymore or working for an owner that doesn't care about you. You will be free. You will own your life.

RYAN: Wow, that's amazing. May I ask a few questions?

THERESA: Yes, of course.

RYAN: What did your parents do for work?

THERESA: Well, my mom works at a pupusa restaurant as a cook, and my dad works as a cook in the Bellagio.

RYAN: Did you go to college or anything?

THERESA: No, I've never been to college. I've worked retail.

RYAN: Wow, do you like retail?

THERESA: No, I don't want to work in the rat race.

RYAN: Have any of the adults in your life had a Roth IRA?

THERESA: (*Looked confused.*) No, I don't think so.

RYAN: Do you work now?

THERESA: Yes, I work at Ross now, but as soon as I finish reading the books my mentor told me to read and we have spent enough time together discussing my goals, then I will be able to travel the world.

RYAN: So, what exactly would I have to do to escape the rat race?

THERESA: Well, I would be your Life Coach, and you would have to Cash App me fifty dollars per session. You would buy the books through me, twenty-five dollars per book. I would let you meet my mentor for one on one sessions, at one hundred dollars per session. We also have a main office that really teaches you how to achieve your goals.

RYAN: How much is that?

THERESA: Three hundred dollars.

RYAN: (*Didn't know what to say.*) That's amazing. So you would be my Life Coach?

THERESA: Yes.

RYAN: What does that mean?

THERESA: We would meet once a week for six weeks, where we discuss your passions and personal life goals. What are your life goals?

RYAN: I currently do not have any.

THERESA: Oh, don't say that. We all have goals in life.

RYAN: I haven't had a goal in a long time.

THERESA: Oh, we have to figure out your passions then.

RYAN: My passions?

THERESA: What are you passionate about?

RYAN: I want to be a bootlegger.

THERESA: (*Looked confused.*) What is a bootlegger?

RYAN: A guy in a really fast car drives illegal alcohol over state lines.

THERESA: Like a drug cartel?

RYAN: Something like that, but you have to have a really fast car.

THERESA: Well, that's a passion. I have some time right now for the first session. Please Cash App me fifty dollars, and I'll be happy to assist you with your dreams.

He pulled out his cell phone and sent her 50 dollars.

THERESA: (*Looking at her phone.*) Okay, I got it. First, you need to make a website. That's how the world knows you are serious and doing business professionally. You need a top notch website that advertises your specific product. Your website needs to provide the details and services your company provides and the prices that go along with each service. Second, you need to get the fast car and make sure it looks great. It is important that your car is always immaculately clean. Clients need to know you are a professional. Respect starts with looking clean and professional. Make sure to have that car detailed and washed regularly, inside and out. Third, a uniform, your uniform, and I don't mean it has to have a slogan, but your everyday dress is a uniform. Pick certain shades of color and stick with them. I always wear a black blazer and a white button-down shirt underneath. You have to recognize that the most successful people of our time, Steve Jobs, Mark Zuckerberg, and Joe Rogan have specific style choices that everyone can recognize instantly. Repeat back to me what I said.

RYAN: First, open a website. Second, clean car. Third, uniform.

THERESA: And finally, have a card. Hand out your card. You never know when you will get a new customer. (*She took a card out of her purse, handed it to Ryan.*)

RYAN: Wow, this is great advice.

THERESA: No problem, Ryan. I'm glad I could help. On the card is my email. Please email me your information, full name, date of birth, social security number, and your address. My mentor likes to have those things.

RYAN: Will do. (*I will never do that.*)
THERESA: (*Standing up.*) Well, I have to go, have a nice day.
RYAN: Bye.

Ryan stared at her card.

RYAN: (*How did I end up spending seventy dollars to go to Starbucks?*)

Chapter 10

In Ryan's quest to learn about what normal people endure on a day to day basis, he posted on Tinder that he would buy single mom's groceries, with no requirement of touching each other or seeing each other again. His only goal was to buy a single mom's groceries.

He received matches for this, but the winner was a 26-year-old Hispanic woman named Esme, short for Esmeralda. Esme had three kids. The first one had been born when she was 17. She had married at 18, but had separated from her husband who was not providing a lot of money to the house. Ryan thought this was the perfect candidate.

Ryan pulled into her apartment complex shortly after the sun went down. It was located on east Lake Mead, almost to Frenchman Mountain. There was a giant Mexican flag hanging from a porch. On another porch there was a giant El Salvadorian flag. Hispanic men were standing by a pickup truck.

He looked around and realized he had never been in this neighborhood. Maybe he had driven through this area before, but for what he couldn't remember. He had never had a reason to be in this part of town. He didn't feel fear. He didn't understand how someone could live in a city all his life and never enter into certain neighborhoods.

He found Esme's apartment and knocked. She opened the door and looked at him. He went inside her apartment. The place was not clean. There were clothes on the floor, kids toys scattered through the apartment, dust on everything. The sink was full of dishes. The kitchen table was covered with marijuana smoking devices.

RYAN: (*What kind of world is this?*)

ESME: (*Walking over to him holding her purse.*) Let's go.

They got into Ryan's 2003 Toyota Corolla. Esme immediately lit up a Camel Crush.

RYAN: (*She is smoking, in my car. Wow. Don't say anything. Let her do it. I don't want her to smoke in my car, but let it happen.*)
ESME: I kicked out my husband. He wouldn't stop. He was always calling me a whore, you know. Like bro, I'm not a whore. Why you have to call me a whore. I swear I'm not doing any whoring.
RYAN: (*She has a California, I-grew-up-with-Spanish-speaking-parents accent.*)
ESME: Now he lives in his truck. That isn't my fault he lives in his truck. He texts me constantly, like twenty times a day. He tells me I'm a whore and I'm a bad mother. He says that I'm selfish and I don't give a shit about our marriage and our kids. He don't do shit, bro. He sits in the house and drinks beer and watches television. I'm young. I know I have kids, but that don't mean I want to sit around in the house all day. I couldn't do anything. If I went out with my friends, he would just call me a whore. I'm not a whore. I've never told anyone to pay me for sex. Shit, bro, I wasted my early twenties on that idiot. I am happy now. I went on a date last Tuesday. I went on a date on Thursday. But it sucks because if I go somewhere, I have to give my sister money to babysit my kids. He is supposed to babysit my kids, but he always has an excuse like he sleeps in his truck and he can't have the kids hang out in his truck for three hours. Like, bro, get an apartment. You know?
RYAN: Yeah, sounds right.
ESME: I know. What's his deal? The other day he brought the kids up to Mount Charleston. They sat in the grass and didn't eat any food. The kids didn't eat all day. Like, can't you feed your kids bro?
RYAN: (*She has absolutely no curiosity regarding who I am or why I am doing this. This lack of curiosity seems dangerous. How does someone get into a car with a stranger from the internet? Does everyone just take giant risks these days? Are risks normalized?*)
ESME: I don't hate my ex; I just don't want him around. I want him to

learn something about himself and get his life together.

RYAN: What do you do Esme?

ESME: Oh, I work reception at a law office. I speak Spanish and most of the clients speak Spanish.

RYAN: Oh good. Are you from Vegas?

Esme: No, I'm from Cali. Couldn't afford to live in Cali anymore, so my family came out here when I was teenager. Wish I could go back to Cali, but it's too expensive.

RYAN: Yeah, it is expensive. So, did you go to any college? (*This was Ryan's default conversation, asking about education.*)

ESME: No, bro. I finished school in eleventh grade. I had to get out of my parents house. My step dad kept grabbing my ass and rubbing my breast. Then he would go and fuck my mom so loud I could hear it. These apartments are small. If someone fucks everyone can hear it. My mom loves fucking. She has seven kids.

RYAN: (*Wow, oh fuck me, seven kids.*) That's a lot of kids.

ESME: Yeah, bro. With six different dudes.

RYAN: Six different dudes?

ESME: Yeah, I told you bro, my mom loves fucking. Fucking strange dudes and letting them cum in her was not a big deal. She just likes fucking. I've heard her get fucked so many times. And, like, bro, a lot of those dudes were creeps. Like two of them would just walk around naked. I was a little kid, man. Shit was fucked. Glad I turned out okay. I got my shit together. I got married. All my kids have the same dad, all three same dad. My mom never did that. She has seven kids, six dads. I have three kids, one dad. And that's all the kids I'm going to have. I'm done. Three is enough.

RYAN: Three is enough. (*She doesn't ask me one question about myself. This is fascinating. She has zero interest in who is talking to her. 11th grade. What does she know. How well can she read? How many states can she name? The world must be dreadfully confusing to her.*) You did a good job having the same dad all three times.

ESME: Yeah, you know. I'm doing pretty good. My mom is fucking stupid.

They arrived at Smith's. The Smith's in Eastern had a cement floor and no Kosher section and a much larger Hispanic section. Esme pushed the cart, Ryan followed. Esme filled the cart full of red soda, pork chops, macaroni and cheese, pre-made cakes, chicken:

ESME: Can I really get anything I want? Can I get beef?
RYAN: Yes.
ESME: (*She threw steaks into the cart.*) I haven't had steaks in years. Can I get cheeseburger meat?
RYAN: Yes.

Esme threw ground beef into her cart.

Esme got chips and crackers, soups, and even instant coffee. Ryan watched her, she looked happy. There was enough food for at least a month.

ESME: How do you cook steak?
RYAN: (*She probably doesn't have a grill.*) You can put it in a skillet and just cook it. You can season it if you want. How do you like your steak?
ESME: Like my steak?
RYAN: Medium-rare or well done?
ESME: Oh, I don't know. I will figure that out, bro.
RYAN: Great.

They paid in line and packed the groceries into the trunk.

Esme closed the door and took a vape marijuana pen from her purse. Ryan watched. She took several hits. Closed her eyes and opened them again.

ESME: I feel better.

They went back to Esme's apartment. Ryan helped bring the groceries inside her house. After the groceries were put away, Esme walked up to Ryan.

ESME: Do you have any cash? I need cigarettes. I only have two left.
RYAN: Yes. (*Took his wallet out and handed her a 20 dollar bill.*)
ESME: Thanks.

Ryan left.

Chapter 11

Ryan decided to hire Theresa as his Life Coach and to be his assistant for his new business of bootlegging. Theresa was happy to take the opportunity. Ryan was the first person she had life-coached.

Theresa and Ryan were at Ryan's house in his garage looking at the Honda Civic Type R. He showed the switch that was put in to turn off the brake lights so he could be invisible at night.

He flicked it.

RYAN: See, all the lights turn off. I will be completely invisible. (*He spoke like an excited child*) I will be able to travel at high speeds through the desert undetected. I'll be able to drive right past the police and they will never know I was there.

THERESA: This is great for business. Your clients will trust your professionalism.

RYAN: I also got these night vision goggles. (*He picked up a helmet type thing with goggles on it, then put it on his head.*) Now, I can drive at night. (*Then, while still wearing the goggles, he picked up a small black box with buttons.*) I have a cop radar. This tells me when cops are around. When the radar detects the cops, I can pull over, turn off the lights, put on the goggles and drive past the cops.

THERESA: This is amazing, Ryan. I can really see that you want to succeed with your business.

RYAN: Thanks Theresa. I've been thinking about it for a long time. Have you ever seen *Smokey and the Bandit*?

THERESA: I don't know. Smokey, and what did you say?

RYAN: It's a movie from the seventies, starring Burt Reynolds.

THERESA: Do you think watching this movie will help me achieve my goals of success and traveling the world? Is that why you are suggesting it?

RYAN: No, (*felt weird now*) merely, hmm. (*Think of something to say or change subject.*) So, how is the website coming along?

THERESA: Fantastic. Let's go inside and look at it.

Ryan and Theresa went inside the house and sat at the kitchen table. Theresa noticed a box with all of Ryan's diplomas.

THERESA: What are those?

RYAN: Those are my diplomas and certificates.

THERESA: You have a lot of them. You must be very successful.

RYAN: (*Ryan looked at the box. I need to move that.*) Sometimes you do things in life, but life keeps happening long after you are done doing those things. After you succeed, you will learn that.

THERESA: I hope I get to one day.

Theresa opened the laptop and showed Ryan the website.

THERESA: See, I had a professional website designer make it. It is specifically designed to be used on the Dark Web just like you wanted.

The website looked contemporary and professional. It said in nice big letters:

Las Vegas Bootlegger

A cool picture of a black Honda Civic Type R with tinted windows. On the top right was three little lines to indicate search.

ABOUT: The Biggest Threat to Secrets is Departments. Las Vegas Bootlegger is a company that provides secrecy. There will be no record of what we are transporting. We have a commitment to trust with our clients. We travel by night under the cover of darkness. There will be no paper trail. No one will ever know that you have requested our services. We do not even have an Excel spreadsheet calculating costs. There are no accounting departments, human resource departments, no departments. We are a business that contains no departments, a departmentless business.

Then there was a What We Provide and Do Not Provide Section.

PROVIDE SECTION: We provide excellent trustworthy service. We meet at a venue of your choosing, you hand over the artifact, we have a small playful conversation that creates a corresponding sense of trust. We take the artifact and deliver it. Imagine us to be an Uber for artifacts.

WHAT WE DO NOT DO: We do not transport drugs or weapons. We transport serious artifacts that demand a unique delivery system.

HOW TO PAY US: Need to know basis.

A Two Minute Video: (*Chopin - Nocturne op. 9. No. 2 plays. Words come across the screen*) Have you wanted Uber for an object? A secret object. An object that demands total secrecy. An artifact of the highest importance. We can transport it. Under the cover of darkness. We are mysterious yet professional people. Excellence is our calling. What is the enemy of secrets? Departments! We have no Excel. We have no accountants. We do not report our taxes. We even transport for the IRS. We believe in trust!

THERESA: I used the word "trust" a lot. It tells people that they can trust us.

RYAN: That's all you have to do is use the word trust and people trust you?

THERESA: Yes. It is important to be trustworthy in today's economy. You have to build relationships of trust.

RYAN: I like the video.

THERESA: It has been shown through focus groups and studies that short videos with dramatic piano music build trust.

RYAN: People will just believe we are trustworthy because of piano music?

THERESA: Yes. I trust anything that uses piano music. I never trust rock and rap.

RYAN: (*I cannot believe anything she is saying. It might be true. I do not want to believe it though. It is okay. What is important is that you do what she says, not that you trust her. Trust is like instant enthusiasm, I think. I am not sure. I think I have trust issues. I do not have any interest in fixing my trust issues. I can pretend I believe. I've always done well at pretending. No one could tell that I wasn't a lawyer, but just a guy who passed a bunch of tests. I fooled everyone and they gave me money.*) This is fantastic Theresa. I'm really impressed on how well you did.

THERESA: (*Smiling.*) (*No one has ever told me I did a good job. I've worked in retail my whole life. No one ever cared how I folded jeans or put clothes on hangers. No one cared when my drawer was perfect. My mother has never told me good job. This is the first time. I should get myself ice cream when I leave to celebrate. The Mentor is really helping. Should I get Cold Stone or Baskin Robbins. Baskin Robbins is on the way home, but Cold Stone is better.*) Thanks Ryan. Is it okay if I put it on the Dark Web now?

RYAN: Yes, of course.

Theresa moved the mouse and clicked a few times.

THERESA: The website is up!

RYAN: I'm really happy. (*I hope someone shoots me during this. Maybe a cop car chase that kills me. I am 39. According to the United State of America Social Security Department, I have approximately 40 years to live. I have already lived 10 years waking up alone on Christmas morning. Ryan often used his mother's Facebook to look at extended family members and people he went to high school with's Facebook pages the day after Christmas. There were many pictures of the family standing around the tree with huge smiles on their faces. He wanted to tell them it was all fake, but it wasn't true;*

they were happy. People woke up next to their spouse on Christmas. It was a thing that happened. Parents shopped for their children on Christmas. They wrapped presents in secret and when the children fell asleep, they snuck out of bed, gathered the presents from a hiding place inside the house and put them under the tree. Ryan would often imagine having a nice wife, an ideal image of his perfect wife, together with her putting the presents under the tree at midnight Christmas Eve. Looking at the presents with her, then looking at her and being in love, a love that made it all worth it. A love that made going to work and taking endless amounts of shit worth it. All the shit of life, from annoying coworkers to chronic illnesses to cleaning the car to getting haircuts to washing the dishes ad nauseam, would become meaningful. His reality would be full of meaning. He would be a hero to a child. Then the person he was in love with and himself would go to sleep cuddling. His arm draped over her midsection, or maybe her arm draped over his midsection. It didn't matter, as long as there was an arm and a midsection. He began to cry quietly, inside his heart. If I have to keep living, in a world where Christmas is a sad event, I do not know what will happen to me. I can barely hold on. I can barely pull it off now. Instead of flowing with life, I keep slipping and falling. Have I committed an act of negligence on my own life, duty breach contract damages. I can't sue myself for what I did and did not do.)

THERESA: I have a uniform for us. Let's go try them on.

Ryan and Theresa went upstairs to his bedroom. There were giant bags of clothes from REI.

Theresa sat in an armchair with the bags next to her. Ryan stood in the room. He went over to pick up the bags, but Theresa stopped him.

THERESA: No, try them on here. I will hand them to you.

RYAN: (*What, I will have no clothes on.*) Okay.

THERESA: This is my plan. You told me you wanted to have a cowboy mixed with a ninteen twenties mysterious look. I don't want you to look weird, like you were in cosplay. People don't trust people in weird cosplay outfits. I went with REI. It is like you are a mountain person, a man of the desert and hiking trails.

RYAN: Cool. Let's see the clothes.

Theresa handed him the first outfit.

RYAN: (*Took his clothes off. Put on the outfit. It was all black and navy blue. There were secret zipper pockets inside the hand pockets. There was a black coat with several zipper pockets.*) I like it.

THERESA: It is comfortable, yet expensive. Clients will understand that you are spending a lot of time in the desert, and they will respect that you need to be comfortable and will probably get dirty.

RYAN: Have you ever seen *Vertigo* where Jimmy Stewart is wearing a suit in the redwood forest?

THERESA: Vertawhat?

RYAN: (*Shit, I did it again.*) It is a movie. These pants fit really well.

THERESA: You look great. You look like a trustworthy person. (*She picked up a bag of undergarments.*) Here, try these on.

RYAN: (*He took the bag. He looked inside.*) These are undergarments. Underwear and long underwear.

THERESA: It will be cold soon. Try them on. (*Theresa sat unrelaxed. She was slightly slouched over, her back arched forward. She lived in a state of crippling anxiety. She had never been able to articulate her emotions or thoughts or ideas. She didn't even know other people could. She didn't even know that she was disabled in this way. She felt no jealousy toward those who could articulate their emotions and ideas. No one in her social circle considered that a thing worth having. She felt dark emotions regarding women who had perfect bodies on Instagram and Tiktok, seeing neighborhoods full of giant houses, seeing people on television that had things she did not have. All of it thrust her body and emotions into a state of upheaval. She didn't understand what caused them to have gained so many things, such large and expensive things, while she had nothing. She was 26, lived with her mother inside a small two room apartment, and drove a 2008 Chevy Cruze that she got at an auction. Her dad had paid for half of it. She wanted to have some power in the world. Just a little, a tiny bit of power. She wanted one person on this entire planet to call her ma'am just once. She didn't understand her life. She didn't understand how one person became important enough to accumulate a nice house with all their bills paid on time and another person ended up at Ross with late bills in an apartment so small the smell of cooked dinner traveled into every room, and one had to go to sleep listening to the sound of a pitbull running across a linoleum floor in the apartment above. She had never noticed, not once, that the bulk of humanity lived similarly to her. It was always her orbiting around those who lived in nice neighborhoods.)*

RYAN: *(He started to walk toward the bathroom.)*

THERESA: No, stay here. I want to see.

RYAN: *(I will be naked in front of her. My penis is super flaccid. Practically retracted. Just do it. Sexuality happens sometimes in the world.)* Okay.

Ryan disrobed. His flaccid penis was approximately two inches. It didn't even dangle. It poked out from his body. Theresa stared at it, but did not show any emotions.

THERESA: You have no skin.

RYAN: Huh.

THERESA: You are circumcised?

RYAN: Yes. I'm American.

THERESA: I've only dated Mexicans and El Salvadorans.

RYAN: Oh.

THERESA: It is so little.

RYAN: I'm a grower not a shower. I've always been embarrassed of it.

THERESA: It looks defenseless, harmless.

RYAN: *(Should I be hurt by that?)*

THERESA: You have tiny balls too. *(Her facial expression seemed more interested than sexy. She did not supply a sexual sign with her eyes.)*

RYAN: Yes.

Ryan tried on the undergarments one after another while Theresa sat in the armchair. After the clothes were all tried on and hung in the closet, Theresa spoke.

THERESA: I have an outfit too, as your assistant I felt it was important to get an outfit.

RYAN: Cool.

THERESA: Okay, sit down. *(She stood, and Ryan sat down in the armchair. She grabbed a bag and stood where Ryan previously changed. She took off her clothes. She felt nervous but she felt compelled. She knew Ryan was harmless. If he was gross, he would have already shown his grossness.)*

RYAN: (Is *this what a naked Mayan looks like. Is she Mayan or am I being racist? I'm probably being racist. She looks nice in the outfit she picked out. It was a juniper green long sleeved button up with matching capri hiking pants.*) You look very trustworthy.

THERESA: That's what I was going for. I've never worn clothes from REI.

Ryan gave her a thumbs up.

Theresa kept her clothes on for the rest of the day. Eventually she received a beep on her phone. Las Vegas Bootlegger had an email.

THERESA: Ryan, we have a customer.

RYAN: (*Oh man. I actually have to do this.*)

THERESA: The pick-up point is in Rachel at the Little A'Le'Inn restaurant. The drop off point is at the Venetian. More information will be provided when you pick up the package.

Chapter 12

The Little A'Le'Inn was two and a half hours north of Las Vegas. Ryan did not travel there under the cover of night. It was lunch time.

Ryan had never been to the Little A'Le'Inn. He had never traveled through Nevada, even though he had lived there his whole life. He had never taken a road trip in his whole life. He didn't study abroad, didn't go to the military and see the world, and he never became an English as Second Language (ESL) teacher in Asia. When he worked as a lawyer, he had the opportunity of doing depositions in Chicago, Boston and New York City, which he enjoyed. His vacations were taken on a plane to Hawaii, Cabo, and the Florida Keys. Wandering around the Earth had never occurred to him, but things had changed inside him. He wanted to wander. The highway seemed like a safe place, in the car by himself. Looking out the window felt special. The desert offered endless mountains and joshua trees to look upon. Sometimes a tumbleweed would fly into the road. He would hit it with his car and feel excited.

He walked into the Little A'Le'Inn restaurant and saw the person he was supposed to meet. She was a woman in her late 30s, around five-foot-three, blond hair, northern European skin, and blue eyes. She was dressed professionally, black pants and blazer, with a gun on her side.

Ryan sat in front of her.

MEL: My name is Mel. Please grab this cup tightly. (*She pointed at a glass in front of him. He grabbed it. Mel's eyes were focused on the cup and his hand.*) Good. (*She picked up the cup and put it in a plastic zip lock bag. She zipped the bag.*) Okay, I have your fingerprints.
RYAN: (*Fuck, she is arresting me.*)

MEL: I'm not arresting you. Okay, let's get things established. I have a gun and I'm in a secret government agency that works at Area 51. I don't feel like driving to Las Vegas. I'm from eastern Pennsylvania, and giant highways scare me. The I-15 infuriates me. I start screaming at everyone, constantly yelling "You fucking idiot!" and honking. I arrive at the casino covered in sweat and pissed as fuck. That's why I need you to do this, okay? Understand?

RYAN: (*Wow, okay.*) Okay.

MEL: I had you put the fingers on the cup because now I have your fingerprints. Here are the expectations for this mission: You deliver the package to Dr. Benway. Here is a picture of him (*She took out the picture showing a southern European man in his late 50s. His nose had red wrinkled lines from decades of alcoholism. He had a bullhorn necklace hanging in dark wiry chest hair.*) His name is not Dr. Benway. That's a code name. He will answer to Dr. Benway though. Okay, now for consequences for a failed mission: If you lose it but it is found, I run your fingerprints and kill you and the person who found it. If you try to run away with it, I kill you and your whole entire family. These are the consequences. They are obviously pretty serious consequences. They told me if I fuck this up, I get killed and my dog. My dog gets killed before me and then I have to watch the dog die. There are rules in the world. We have to follow them or there is chaos. Do you understand?

RYAN: I understand. Does the United States Government often resort to murder?

Mel: Are you an idiot? There are three hundred and thirty million people, losing a few is not a big deal. (*She sincerely looked at him like he was an idiot.*)

RYAN: (*I have to stop asking dumb questions.*)

MEL: (*She brought out a grey plastic case the size of a shoebox. She opened the box and picked up an eight-inch phallic, metal and black device with a tiny one-inch disc at one end. She held in the air so Ryan could look at it.*) See, this is it. It shoots emotions.

RYAN: It looks like Anakin Skywalker's lightsaber.

MEL: I know, right. It is awesome. It isn't a lightsaber though. It shoots emotions. Well, not really emotions. At first, we wanted to make a machine that you shot at people and made emotions, but that's not how emotions work. See, emotions don't exist. Like this restaurant exists (*Motioned with arms and hands.*) It is true that we have similar emotions to similar stimuli, but emotions and moods exist like the element flerovium. They exist inside the body and then disappear leaving no trace of their existence. Have you ever been extremely happy, then suddenly something happens and you switch to anger and frustration? Where did the happiness go? It just disappeared. That's how emotions work. Our nerds tell us that emotions exist when triggered. You have to tap the brain, and then emotions arise in the body. We realized the best way to do that is through music, so we decided to take versions of songs and concentrate them into one second, then shoot that second at a person, with no noise. It is totally silent. Then we had to choose the songs. I loved that. There were days upon days of us sitting around doing nothing, just getting paid to write song names on a dry erase board. I love work days that are just meetings. Man, I love a good meeting. This was like two weeks of meetings. Well, we picked three songs. One: Sam Cooke's "Having a Party." This was a happy song. You get shot with this, your heart becomes pure for at least ten minutes. You start dancing and you live in the moment. I love getting shot with "Having a Party." The second is Bach's "Chaconne" performed by Hilary Hahn into a shot. This one can destabilize everyone. It forces them to reflect on something they put a lot of effort into that did not turn out the way they thought it would. If shot with this, people will reflect upon their failed marriage, a child that died, something they thought they would accomplish but fell through, and the fact in general that they will die a stupid death one day.

RYAN: A stupid death?

MEL: We all die stupid deaths. Then we did Pearl Jam's "Black," the MTV unplugged version. This is sadness but with forgiveness. The human will scream like a maniac when faced with rejection by another person, but sometimes they understand and let it happen. In life we need that, even if it is just a lie.

RYAN: (*This is the coolest moment of my life.*)

MEL: We do not know what to do with it. At first we thought we could make rioters have emotional breakdowns, but we shot it into crowds, and we learned that any emotion, happy or sad, if a large group of people are experiencing the same emotion at the same time, unifies them and makes them more violent. People can become violent with both happy and sad emotions. We learned that group violence requires some level of fun. The violence is a party to the rioters.

RYAN: For riots not war?

MEL: The future is riots. We do not have money for wars any longer. That ship has sailed. So, the song shooter doesn't work on rioters. We are going to try to sell to it Amazon or Apple. We think maybe they can use it as a way to sell more products. As people are looking at the Amazon website, secretly a song is shot from the speaker into their body and it makes them impulsive and self-loathing at the same time in order to get them to buy things they don't need. We do not know which song would do that. Our job was only to create an emotion shooter and to test it on riot crowds, not to test it for private sector purposes. Whoever buys it, Amazon or Apple, will have to figure that out.

RYAN: Would you shoot me?

MEL: I don't care. It only lasts five minutes. Which song?

RYAN: The "Chaconne."

MEL: Oh, you want to see something. I like a man who isn't afraid of danger. (*She pointed the lightsaber looking device at Ryan and pressed a button.*)

RYAN: (*His face instantly changed.*)

MEL: (*I can see it in his face. It is beautiful.*)

RYAN: It is like I feel my disappointment, and I know exactly why I am disappointed, and even though I don't want to be feeling these emotions, I am very conscious of how selfish I have been in life, but I can't stop myself. I know that luck is real and I can't deny it. Luck is a thousand times more real than effort. I mean, is luck God's Grace? God does actually care, but He cares in a way that is ineffable. Even in my most stupid and sinful of moments, there was still a moment that seemed lucky and warm. A falling feeling has come over me. I can see that I have made other people endure unpleasant things also. It wasn't just them; I was being a dick also. Now is waiting, waiting and enduring, feeling listless, wondering when the next worthwhile thing will happen, scared that nothing good will ever happen in your life again. What if I die without ever falling in love or having sex again? Then it breaks. Something good has happened again. As you get older, it isn't as easy to start again, to believe again, yet we do it. All of us do it again and again. If I feel like this way forever, I will have to kill myself to end it.

MEL: Oh, good. I'm glad you did it.

RYAN: (*Visibly shaken.*) Yes, it was painful, but I'm glad I did it.

MEL: (*She put the item back into the box and slid the box over to him.*) Dr. Benway will be sitting at a black jack table at 8:30 p.m. tonight. Just sit next to him, make conversation, and hand him the case.

Mel stood up, paid her bill, and walked out.

Chapter 13

Ryan entered the Venetian to find Dr. Benway. Ryan never went to the Strip, unless he wanted to go to a buffet, which hardly ever happened. He didn't think about it. It was something in his city, the way Disney Land exists in Los Angeles. He looked around the Venetian.

RYAN: (*There are so many people. What are they doing here? What do they want?*) (*He saw people gambling. Sitting peacefully, hitting the slot machine buttons. All the races/nationalities/religions of the world gambling. Is that a good thing? Is Las Vegas bringing the world together? Is Las Vegas creating world peace?*)

He took the picture of Dr. Benway out of his pocket and looked at it. Then he looked up to see if he could find him. He walked aimlessly through the casino for 20 minutes until he found Dr. Benway sitting at a poker table.

He tapped Dr. Benway on the shoulder.

DR. BENWAY: (*Looked up at Ryan's face. Then looked at his hands to see if he was carrying the box.*) I will stop playing. Then let's go. I have something to show you.

Ryan stepped back a few feet and waited. He felt nervous. This was an older, excessively confident man. He reminded him of the older attorneys he used to work with.

Dr. Benway stood and motioned with his hand to follow him. They walked amongst the crowds and noise. A sound of a hawk call and a buffalo stampede were constant, coming from the slot machines.

As they entered the elevator, Dr. Benway started talking.

DR. BENWAY: Attorney Neroni, I can see you've changed your life.

RYAN: Yes, a life change.

DR. BENWAY: You and I are a lot alike. I grew up in a nice family in Brooklyn. My parents were both college-educated and loving. I was always competent, and I loved being perceived as competent and trustworthy. Everyone trusted me (*Said in a funny voice, mocking his own life.*) It was all I had, my amazing competence. I always got perfect grades. I excelled in math, science, history, and English. I was attractive and athletic. I was a champion on the college campus. I loved school. I have an M.D., a D.O, and a Ph.D. regarding the brain/neurology. What kind of person does that? In my late thirties/ early forties I operated on the Pope and several famous politicians and business leaders. It started to bother me though. It all felt like luck. I felt like a faker. I started drinking, not a beer before I went to bed, but booze and ice, like I was some kind of fucking cowboy or something. You know, when you are young you don't know anything, as in, young people just don't know. I had this affection, though, for being esteemed by my professors. Every compliment I received from my professors fed and nourished me. I would call my mom and tell her the compliment the profesor paid me, and she screamed with joy. That woman really loves me, but damn she was always up my ass. My parents loved me too much. Sometimes I wish they loved me a little less, so I could have done what I wanted with my life.

RYAN: (*Wow, he talks a lot.*)

DR. BENWAY: I loved school. It is fair. You show up to class and take notes and the one with the genetically superior memory wins. I had the genetically superior memory. After I finished every possible degree, I had to work. I had to leave the campus and open my own business. I didn't want to run a business, but that's what they told me I had to do. I did what everyone told me to do. It made everyone happy. Then I started drinking. My hands started shaking and my wife left me. She left and I didn't even feel sad about it. I was like "Okay." She married me for all the wrong reasons. I knew that because I lived my life for all the wrong reasons. I didn't feel like I was helping anyone. I knew I was scamming insurance companies and Medicaid, which are there, in a way, to be scammed. I didn't feel like a doctor. I drank more. My hands began to shake, and I couldn't do surgeries. Everyone knew the golden boy was fucking everything up. I started taking pain killers, and things got even worse. I ended up at a deposition for one of my patients, you know, to give causation, saying that the injury was caused by said accident. I was up the entire night before in the casino drinking and taking Adderall. What kind of forty-something year old man takes Adderall?

RYAN: I don't know. Sounds bad.

DR. BENWAY: Yes, very bad. Well, I went to the deposition and told them I was Bugs Bunny when they asked for my name. I couldn't stop laughing. The deposition had to be cancelled. I got into a lot of trouble for that. After the trouble settled down, people from Area 51 came to me and said, "We know you are the best and you are a free agent now. Would you like to work for us? No surgeries, no running a business. We will give you a nice house in the desert. We know what you need, peace from the world." I took it. I went to Area 51 ten years ago. See, Attorney Neroni, you aren't the only one. There are others that were as lucky as you, and they told that luck to fuck itself.

RYAN: Yes. We are the lucky ones.

DR. BENWAY: Don't kill yourself. The world does need people like us. They just don't need us to contrive ways to fuck them out of their money.

RYAN: (*Laughed.*)

Standing before a hotel door.

DR. BENWAY: Before we go in, please emotionally prepare yourself. There is something in the hotel room that you have never seen before in your entire life and will probably never see again.

RYAN: (*This just got awesome. I wonder what it is. Let it happen. Just let the experience happen. Okay, what does it mean to prepare oneself? Get out of your head, look around, breathe, feel your breath, relax your arms, legs and anus muscles.*) Okay. I'm ready.
DR. BENWAY: Okay, this is really exciting.

Dr. Benway opened the door and they both entered the room. There were two twin beds in the room. There was a man dressed in a suit sitting in an armchair. Both of his arms were on the arms of the chair, his legs uncrossed, with a serious facial expression. His eyes were open. He was not moving.

RYAN: (*Still standing.*) (*Why isn't that person moving? What the fuck is this? He looks about 45, Korean, possibly. This is the coolest moment of my life.*)
DR. BENWAY: (*He sat on a bed and looked at the immobile man.*) Have a seat Attorney Neroni.

Ryan sat on the other twin bed. He couldn't take his eyes off the immoble man.

DR. BENWAY: We call him Randall Flagg.
RYAN: After the Stephen King character.
DR. BENWAY: Yes. We thought of many names. It was a three-day meeting. Other names that were suggested were Nosferatu, the Wandering Jew, and Fosca. Nosferatu was too scary, the Wandering Jew a little too religious, and Fosca too obscure.
RYAN: I don't know the Fosca reference at all.
DR. BENWAY: It is a character that lives forever in a Simone de Beauvoir novel. We settled on Randall Flag because it is Las Vegas. (*Dr. Benway stared at Randall Flagg with a small smile.*) On October first, 2017, on the night of the shooting, every hotel room was inspected by the police. When the police opened the door, they found him sitting right there. He has been there for over two years now. Peacefully sitting there. Sands Corp who owns the Venetian didn't know what to do. The police told them it wasn't their problem. He is alive and

not doing anything bad and we obviously have bigger problems now. Sands Corp closed off the room. No one could go in. Then they contacted somebody, I don't know, and I was sent here in December of 2017. I've been here ever since. My job is to take his temperature and pulse three times a day.

RYAN: He doesn't eat or go to the bathroom?

DR. BENWAY: No, no eating, no bathroom. He only sits and stares. When I was first assigned this task, I did tests. His fingerprints led nowhere. We did a genetic test, like a 23andme, he has no genetic markers. He doesn't exist. It is like he just appeared in our reality. We contacted older institutions of record keeping to see if they had any record of a man showing up after a tragic accident and not leaving. The Vatican said "Do not attempt to kill or move him, but that is all the information we will give." We asked an old Rabbi. Same thing, don't kill or move. We asked China, and they said they got one right now in Chongqing. They said the Buddhists told them not to kill or try to move it. So we've let it stay right there in that chair. We think there are no records of it for the same reason we are not keeping a record of it. It is too weird. You can't put something like this into the annual budget. Do you have the emotion gun?

RYAN: Yes, I forgot. (*He handed the box to Dr. Benway.*)

DR. BENWAY: (*He opened the box and picked up the device.*) It looks like a fancy vibrator or Anakin Skywalker's lightsaber. Cool.

RYAN: Yeah, it looks like Anakin Skywalker's lightsaber.

DR. BENWAY: I'm going to shoot myself with it to see if it works.

RYAN: Mel shot me. It works.

DR. BENWAY: I'm going to do Sam Cooke's "Having a Party". Which one did you do?

RYAN: The "Chaconne."

DR. BENWAY: I don't need that shit. (*He pointed the lightsaber at his chest and pressed the button.*)

Dr. Benway laid back on the bed, and tears crept out of his eyes.

DR. BENWAY: I am in college, undergrad. Molly Murphy, an Irish beauty,

I feel my penis inside her. I can hear her making little noises. My arms are around her. I am in the moment. It feels like eternity. I am happy. (*Dr. Benway had a zen like smile on his face.*) I am ejaculating on her chest. She looks so happy to see me cum.

RYAN: (*Wow, I want to do that one.*)

DR. BENWAY: It was like I was there. I was not here. I was truly there. I was really twenty years old again. A person could get addicted to a thing like this. (*He held up the device.*) Sam Cooke was the best. I would love a greatest hits collection for this. You like Sam Cooke?

RYAN: I like "Another Saturday Night."

DR. BENWAY: Seriously Attorney Neroni, have you tried online dating?

RYAN: Thanks.

DR. BENWAY: Laughs. So this is Mel's plan. She told me to shoot Randall Flagg with the lightsaber. First if it moves, it moves, and second if it does not move, I'm supposed to check its pulse. I'll shoot it with "Having a Party."

Dr. Benway pointed the emotion shooter at Randall Flag and pressed the button. Dr. Benway and Ryan waited in anticipation for something to happen.

Nothing happened.

DR. BENWAY: Nothing happened. Let me take its pulse and blood pressure. (*Dr. Benway performed said duties.*) Nothing.

RYAN: What if it never moves? Is there a movement deadline?

DR. BENWAY: If it doesn't move by 2021, we will shoot it into space. Space Force will perform experiments on it in zero gravity. If it still doesn't move, they will throw it into space like garbage. We can't have it on the planet.

Chapter 14

The next mission involved driving to Anthem in Henderson, Nevada. Ryan had never gone to Anthem. It was on the far southeast corner of Las Vegas. He had known lawyers who lived there, but no one else. It never seemed like a real place, like a dream on the edge of Las Vegas.

It was 9 at night and dark. He got off the highway at the M Casino and went east. It became immediately pitch black following the GPS.

RYAN: (*Is Anthem real?*)

He eventually made it to streets where there were lights.

RYAN: (*This doesn't look like Las Vegas at all, more like a suburb of Chicago.*)

There were playgrounds and parks every few blocks. It was a utopia for children and families. It was the kind of place to raise a family. Ryan would never raise a family. He didn't like it.

Ryan found the house where the package was. It was a large ranch house. He walked to the door and felt nervous. He pressed the doorbell.

A man the same age as Ryan opened the door. He was wearing exercise pants, an old t-shirt, and a robe. His hair was a little long and messy. He was obviously in sleepy clothes. The man said hello and motioned for him to follow him. The man closed the door.

A woman was playing the piano, a mini-grand piano. The man stood watching her. Ryan stood with him looking at her play. The woman never looked up.

ANDREW: My name is Andrew, that's my wife, Xiao. She is playing Chopin's Opus Fifty-five, Number one in F Minor Andante. She has been playing it for hours. She likes to practice. I don't know where she goes when she practices, but I assume it is a happy place. She won't bother us, don't worry. Come follow me.

Andrew walked to a door, he opened it slowly. A child was sleeping in the bed.

ANDREW: Kids are cute when they are asleep.
RYAN: (*I know nothing about children. Think of an appropriate question.*) How old is he?
ANDREW: Seven.

Andrew closed the door and motioned for Ryan to follow him. He pointed at a couch.

ANDREW: Please take a seat. (*Andrew sat on an armchair. He crossed his legs and looked relaxed and confident.*) The Committee checked on you. I know your history and your life facts. You and I are about the same age. Both class of 1999.
RYAN: Yes.
ANDREW: Very different lives we have led. I met Xiao shortly after moving to Las Vegas five years ago. I started working at the university and wanted to get laid. That was my only intention, to go on Ok-Cupid and get laid. I went on a date with her, then I felt really sorry for her. She worked at a preschool for Asians in Chinatown making thirteen dollars an hour. She had a music degree from Chongqing University, but her English sucked then, and it still sucks, so she can't get a job teaching American kids. She had a kid, and I wanted to do something nice and married her. (*She also gave good blowjobs.*) We were married. I am surprised I did that. I have often thought about leaving, but the day passes and I return to this same house. We don't even talk that much, maybe every few days. I spend time with the kid everyday. He calls me Daddy. I never knew I wanted

to be called Daddy. I am addicted to it now. Him not being my kid takes off some of the pressure. Less to live up to. She spends too much time in her bedroom and alone. She often has crying fits. Her story is really shitty and I've never quite understood it. Something like, regarding the one child policy, being sent to a village to live with her grandparents, and I am pretty sure her grandpa fucked her. She won't say that, but it seems implicit. This is how my life turned out.

RYAN: She is pretty.

ANDREW: I don't think she knows that. I don't know what she knows. I don't know what I know. Can I ask you something, have you begun to suspect that the world is wacky?

RYAN: That things are really bad, and maybe things have always been really bad, but you don't become conscious of it until your late thirties.

ANDREW: Yes. Like, one day you are in the car and it hits you, wow, things are really messed up. I'm messed up. I've always been messed up. I am a fucking disaster. My wife is a disaster. My mother is a disaster. My best friend is a disaster. One of the worst things is that for me, and I think this might be a twenty-first century realization. It doesn't feel like it has meaning, that God supplies meaning, but also it doesn't feel like there is no meaning either.

RYAN: Like meaning and lack of meaning was just a game. A game that finished, a game that played itself out.

ANDREW: It feels like we are at the end of the world.

RYAN: Sometimes my only hope to redeem this life I have been given is to go to the Barnes and Nobles Starbucks and look at this cashier. She has grey hair. She colors it like an old woman. When she makes my coffee, she turns around and I look at her butt. I have a degree from the University of Chicago, I have attended hours upon hours of Catholic masses, I have done trials in front of juries, serious, life achievements, and none of it provides enough emotional impact to get me through the years, so I go to Starbucks inside Barnes and Nobles and look at a woman's butt. What if we have built this entire civilization, destroyed vast amounts of the planet, and heated it up, but all we want to do is look at butts and play out our issues with our parents? We could have done that with less environmental destruction. I really like butts. I have liked butts since I was a teenager. I know you are supposed to accomplish things in life, but I don't know anymore.

ANDREW: Everything I do is for Xiao's butt and her kid. (*He looked off, 300 yard stare.*) When I was young I thought I was a good person. I used to yell at people in bars about their political opinions. I used to announce to people I was a communist or anarchist. I had a million ways that I wanted to be identified. I'm not a good person, though. I mean, I'm not good at being a person. There are people who have full-time jobs, plus they volunteer, donate to charity, and mountain-bike all in one week. I barely make it to work. I take care of a child that is not my own. That is my penance for spending the better part of my adulthood drinking and yelling at people in bars. You know why I like Xiao? She doesn't have one political opinion. She has no idea how politics works, nor does she care. I'm an English professor on a college campus. All day I hear political opinions. They discuss political opinions like the Byzantines talked about the Trinity. (*He put his face into his palms and rubbed.*) People are starved to have identity. They want to have something, screaming "This is all I have, this is all I have!" People want to feel important, and it kills them that they are brutally dispensable. Opinions have become the currency buying you into jobs, tenure, and relationships. I went hiking the other day on Mount Charlston, and there were these two guys and two women. They were in a truck with a blue lives matter flag, and I'm like, "Oh my God, what is this? How is this a real thing? Why would anyone think loving cops is cool? " One of my students told me that Newtonian Physics had to be thrown out because Newton never had children or got married. His meals and housekeeping were completely taken care of by Cambridge. His distance from the life of a woman was too great, so he has to be disregarded. She wasn't a science major; she was a sociology major. She said it had to be done for social purposes. Rich people have no problem with global warming. We've been talking about national health insurance since the nineties. I don't know what is wrong with me, I feel like I woke up one day-

RYAN: And you weren't supposed to be there. You didn't know how to be cool anymore.

ANDREW: I know this sounds horrible. This all sounds like a stupid man, a stupid man who can't figure it out. I mean, I have compassion for the fact that people desperately want a piece of the world. They want representation, but our emotions make us so stupid. I remember being an atheist when I was a teenager and feeling fucking cool announcing it the to Christian kids. There is nothing fucking cool about being an athiest. It is like saying "I am a plant." There isn't anything cool about being on par with a plant. Hello my name is Andrew I'm a fucking plant. There isn't anything cool about denying the religion of millions, sucking a cop's dick, or denying gravity because it looks good on your Instagram. I'm so happy I get to come home to a wife that doesn't even know who the president is.

RYAN: She doesn't know who the president is?

ANDREW: She has never mentioned him.

RYAN: Wow. (*Trump disturbed him. He was the powerful leader of self-importance. There was no stopping him in his narcissistic path to rule the empire of self-importance. When Ryan heard Trump's voice on the TV, he would flee the area, like a smelly wet fart had been gooped into the world. The only president he liked during his lifetime was Obama. He didn't think he was a master of policy or anything, just a generalized okayness for his presidency. He thought the Clintons were scamming-ass bitches that used the United States federal government as their own personal oil well. He never thought about Bush. He was too busy being in college in those years to have taken note of the outside world and its goings ons.*) (*I have to get out of this conversation.*) What about that package?

ANDREW: She doesn't let me eat bananas after 7 p.m.

RYAN: What bananas?

ANDREW: She thinks it hurts you. She has all kinds of superstitions. I have to follow all of them.

RYAN: You love her though, right?

ANDREW: Even though I think she is completely irrational, I feel compelled to protect her and make sure she can play the piano as much as she wants. That's love, right?

RYAN: I'm pretty sure that is textbook love.

ANDREW: Okay, I was worried. Sometimes I get worried I am full of shit. You know, full of shit.

RYAN: (*This guy needs to see a therapist.*)

ANDREW: (*He picked up a zip lock bag containing a book. He handed it to Ryan. Ryan held it with both hands looking at it.*) It is a first edition copy of Joyce's Ulysses. First edition copies usually have a number, but this one has no number. It is the copy purchased by Hemingway, himself. It has been passed around for over a hundred years now. At one point Fitzgerald had it, then Norman Mailer had it on his shelf for years. Then it got passed along until it made it to the Committee. The Committee keeps these books in secret. If you are a writer or professor you can keep one of their books for two months, but then you have to return it. They are kept in Tonopah at Whitney's Bookshelf. The books cannot be mailed. That's why I am asking you to do this. It must be returned tomorrow, or the Committee will send out their agents. I have no desire to deal with angry alcoholic lit nerds. They will probably talk to me to death about metaphors and allegories. (*He laughed. Ryan remained silent.*) The bookstore opens at 11 a.m. tomorrow morning. If you leave now you can make it. I have booked you a hotel room at Tonopah Station. There is a large bear there. You will like it.

RYAN: I should get a move on then.

ANDREW: I'll be here with Chopin, my Chinese Chopin. Rubinstein, all night. A thousand years of Rubinstein.

RYAN: (*What is a Rubinstein?*)

When Ryan left, Xiao was still practicing Chopin on the piano.

Ryan drove under the cover of darkness north on I-95 to Tonopah. According to the GPS it took three hours and seven minutes. He wanted to go to sleep in a nice hotel room with a bear. He did not ask Ryan what he meant by bear. He did not care anymore about predicting the future. He was sure there was a bear, but what form it was going to take did not matter to Ryan. Maybe it was a person nicknamed bear, maybe a live bear, he did not know. He did not want to predict or know or ruin his present moments with certainty. Certainty was boring to him. That's why he had become a trial lawyer, to defeat certainty.

Halfway to Tonopah, his radar detector went off. It went beep beep beep. Ryan pulled his car over to the side of the road. He flipped the switch that controlled the lights. All the lights went off. Even if he pressed on the brake, the brake lights would not turn on. He put on his night vision goggles. He was ready.

It was 11:30 p.m. The desert was dark. The stars were visible. There was silence for 100 miles around, except for lizards scurrying through sagebrush and jackrabbits hopping on desert sand. Ryan's car was going about 120 mph when he passed the police car. The officer in the car looked at the radar and it read 123 mph. The officer jumped up in his seat, looking for a car, but there was none there. Not a car in sight. He looked at the radar, reading 123 mph. The officer called dispatch.

OFFICER: I think something blew by me at a hundred and twenty-three mph.
DISPATCH: What, really?
OFFICER: Yeah, but it was invisible.
DISPATCH: Seriously, cool.
OFFICER: Right, how cool is that?
DISPATCH: You seriously didn't see anything.
OFFICER: I saw nothing.
DISPATCH: Well, you aren't going to catch it from a dead stop even if you see it.
OFFICER: I hope whatever it was doesn't run over too many jackrabbits.
DISPATCH: Gotta watch for those jackrabbits.
OFFICER: Jackrabbits will get you in the middle of the night.

Ryan was happy. He had done it. He knew cops could not stop him. He pulled over and took off his night vision goggles and turned his lights back on. He was almost there and wasn't worried anymore about speeding. He took it easy that last hour to Tonopah.

He pulled into Tonopah. It didn't seem like a real place. A man was standing outside in the darkness. He was looking for cigarettes on the ground and in the garbage cans. There were no other people. Ryan parked his car at Tonopah Station. He got out of his car and stood in the desert night. He loved it. All his life he had lived in the desert but had never bothered to care about it.

RYAN: (*I didn't live in the desert, I lived in my head. I lived for a program that ruled my ambitions. My ambition now is to be like a jackrabbit, a desert lizard, a bighorn sheep.*) (*For the first time in Ryan's life he felt truly romantic. He felt like a poet. Not a real poet, of course, who spends their days trying to win awards and get tenure. The imagined poet that lives inside everyone's hearts.*) .

He walked into Tonopah Station. It was an old west museum/casino/hotel/restaurant. He felt like his dreams had come true. He went to the desk. A middle-aged white woman was sitting watching a movie on her laptop. She looked up at him standing behind the desk. She touched the mouse and hit pause on the show she was watching.

DESK CLERK: I was watching my K-drama, you like K-dramas? (*Smiling.*)
RYAN: (*I like this woman.*) I've seen a few. I watched one called The Possessed recently.
DESK CLERK: Oh, that one was good. It was really funny. I love how in K-dramas love is real and eventually everyone gets a chance to redeem themselves.
RYAN: Yes, redemption is cathartic.
DESK CLERK: Do you have a room already or are you booking one now?
RYAN: I have one booked. My name is Ryan Neroni.
DESK CLERK: Mr. Neroni. (*Looking.*) Okay, I found it.

The Desk Clerk handed over the key. It was a real key and not just a card.

RYAN: Is it okay if I looked around?

DESK CLERK: The casino is open all night. The restaurant is closed now,
    but it opens at 8 a.m.
RYAN: Okay.

Ryan walked through the museum and there it was, the bear. It was
a giant stuffed bear standing 10 feet high. He stood in front of the bear
and admired it. He wanted to touch it.

DESK CLERK: (*Yelling.*) That's James the Bear.
RYAN: I love it.
DESK CLERK: That's why I work here, because of James the Bear. I just
    feel warm inside being near James the Bear.
RYAN: I feel like every choice I've ever made has led me to James the
    Bear.
DESK CLERK: James the Bear can save you.
RYAN: I hope he does.

Ryan went to his room. The room was basic. Nothing special about
it. Ryan went to sleep.

The next day Ryan woke up and didn't feel completely rested. He
packed his stuff, and three times he checked to make sure his phone
charger was in his bag. He had a problem with leaving things in hotel
rooms, especially phone chargers.

He ate breakfast at the hotel restaurant and then walked to the
bookstore. The sky was empty of clouds. The sunlight was everywhere,
the pale blue sky covering the landscape like a dome. It made sense to
Ryan that the sky and ocean were blue and hardly anything on land was
completely blue. If things on land were blue, we wouldn't be able to see
things. This was one of Ryan's Proofs of God. Another of his proofs was
not as cute. It was that people and animals were stupid; they couldn't
possibly live. Therefore, God was helping everyone a little bit all the
time. His last proof was charming and his favorite: that most people
viewed all the bad shit as proof God did not exist, but for Ryan, reality was perfectly designed for charitable and loving acts. The fact that
there was so much suffering guaranteed that good deeds could be done

constantly. Ryan never told anyone his thoughts on the subject of God's proofs. He knew he was a master of argument. He had won many motions and trials in his life. He could make logic and points where no one could. He knew he had a talent for logic and deconstructing arguments and building his own argument out of the argument he just destroyed. He knew every logical fallacy by heart. He could spot them instantly and destroy them. Therefore, he did not trust his own ability to create logic because he knew he was so good at it.

At exactly 11 a.m. Ryan went into the bookstore.

RYAN: (*Wow, it smells like dust in here.*)

There was a young Black woman behind the counter. She was wearing a lot of make-up, very well done. Large hoop earrings and a nose ring. The nose ring had a chain that went from her nose to her ear. The chain was a bright silver that contrasted with her dark brown skin. There was a tattoo of flowers around her left eye.

YOUNG WOMAN: Do you need anything?
RYAN: I have a book to drop off.
YOUNG WOMAN: Follow me.

The young woman with the face tattoo walked to the back of the bookstore. Ryan followed.

She opened a door with a key and went into a dark room that was even dustier than the bookstore.

RYAN: (*I will need to Neti Pot soon.*)
YOUNG WOMAN: Hand me the book.

Ryan put the book, still inside the Ziplock bag, into her hands. She inspected it to see if it was the right book. She moved a curtain and exposed an ancient looking bank vault. She put in a code and turned the anchor and the door opened.

The room was full of books.

YOUNG WOMAN: This was a bank a hundred years ago. The safe is a leftover from that time. No one knows it was a bank though. It was scrubbed from the city records. The room is temperature and humidity controlled. I have to come back here every day and open the books and lightly flip through the pages of every book, so the spines don't rot into place.
RYAN: (*Looking around. This is fucking cool.*)

The young woman put the book back.
They walked back to the front of the store. The young woman went behind the counter and picked up a book. She walked over to Ryan, who was just looking around at things.
The young woman handed Ryan a book, *The Savage Detectives* by Roberto Bolaño.

YOUNG WOMAN: It is about poets and cars and crazy times. You might like it.
RYAN: (*Holding the book.*) Thank you.
YOUNG WOMAN: You can have it for free. You are now an esquire of literature.
RYAN: I'm an esquire?
YOUNG WOMAN: Yes, you have done your duty and protected the history of literature.
RYAN: That sounds great.

Ryan walked out of the bookstore holding his copy of *The Savage Detectives*.

Chapter 15

The next mission required Theresa, a long drive to Tucson, and the love between two women.

Theresa and Ryan parked the Honda Civic Type R outside a house in southwest Las Vegas. A nice neighborhood, not as nice as Anthem, but still a nice place to raise a family.

A woman in her early 30s let them in. She was about five-four, with the body of a gymnast, big dark brown curly hair, and eyebrows like Elizabeth Taylor's. It was not a porn or movie star beauty, something else, something unique, maybe old Hollywood. Theresa and Ryan were impressed with her beauty.

The woman sat at her kitchen table and motioned for them to sit down.

TASHA: My name is Tasha, what are your names? (*She seemed sad. She didn't want to talk about what she was going to talk about.*)

RYAN: Ryan and this is Theresa, my assistant.

THERESA: Hi.

TASHA: (*She put her hand on a pair of sunglasses and underwear on the table. The underwear was in a zip lock bag.*) I want you to give these two items to a woman in Tucson. Her name is Diane Butler, she is like a lesbian country-folk musician. She is kind of famous. She had a Tiny Desk Concert a year ago. Have you heard of her?

RYAN: No. Is that like Rail Yard Ghosts?

TASHA: Kind of like that. Same fans basically.

THERESA: I only listen to music in Spanish.

TASHA: (*She never looked Ryan or Theresa in the eyes. She kept biting her nails.*)

I have not seen Diane in seven years. I have lied to myself so much about her, and I can't lie anymore. When we broke up she wrote letters and texted for six months. My friends told me she was a stalker bitch, that was she was creepy and mentally ill. I agreed with my friends. It made things easier to write off Diane as a stalker and mentally ill. Diane eventually stopped writing to me. A year passed, and she sent me an audio file of her new album. It was eight songs, all about me. Her big hits were on it. Every song was about our love and me. I inspired her. I was her muse. She broke into a thousand pieces because she could not hold me, because I refused to make her laugh. I would do nothing for her anymore and I made sure she knew I would never need her again. I don't know why, but I just couldn't believe that I could be so special to anyone, especially someone that could make such beautiful music. People in reviews called her a genius. (*Tears started.*) I loved a genius and a genius loved me.

RYAN: (*Here it comes.*)

TASHA: I cheated on her, several times, and I even let her catch me. I let her catch me in the most distrustful act. I couldn't go back after that. (*She got louder.*) How could I face her? My friends told me she was crazy, she would never be a famous rich musician, she didn't have a mom, her mom was a drug addict that overdosed and died. She was never going to have a normal life, she believed only in one thing, music (*pause*) and me. She was so full of passion, heart and love. When we made love, she gave it all to me. All of her creativity and passion struck me. It crashed into me. Her hands on my body felt electric, her legs wrapped around me, it felt like home, her lips on mine, and her hands... When I am crying and having a rough day, I hold out my hand and say, "Diane, hold my hand, please," and she does. I can feel her hand in mine like it is real. Sometimes it feels truly real, like she is right beside me. She isn't though. (*Pause.*) I wanted a good future. I grew up here in Las Vegas with a card dealer mother and a truck driver dad and several siblings in a little ranch house off Charleston. My mother constantly told me that I had to make something of my life, go to college, do this, do that. My parents worked hard for me to have a better life, a two-story house in a good neighborhood. My friends never stopped reminding me that Diane was never going to provide this. I believed them. I broke up with Diane. I got drunk and had sex with several people. You know break-up party girl blues. One of the rebounds is now my wife, Ashley. My friend introduced me to her. She comes from a normal two-parent family that lives in Summerlin. Her dad is a doctor and her mom works for the state. They have a wonderful house. We have wonderful Christmasses. My parents love her. All my friends love her. She's a respiratory therapist and makes eighty thousand dollars a year. We have this great house. A nice two-story house in a nice neighborhood. My family could never pay for half a wedding. I had a beautiful wedding because of Ashley's family. (*She pointed at wedding photos. The photos were beautiful.*)

THERESA: (*It is a nice house.*)

TASHA: I got everything I ever wanted out of life. I won. (*Pause.*) Not a day passes where I don't think of Diane. Not a single day. She haunts me. I miss her. I really miss her, but I can't turn back now. I have done horrible things and there is no redemption for me. My guilt is too deep. I can't be in the same room with her ever again.

RYAN: (*Like Anakin Skywalker after he killed the younglings.*)

TASHA: I just couldn't believe that someone could love me so much. I'm a truck driver's daughter. I'm nobody. I'm a sixth grade teacher. I'm not anybody. I have no talent. There is nothing great about me. How could someone that contained such talent and persistence to live out her dream of being a musician want to stand next to me? I mean, society tells you a two-story house in a nice neighborhood is the dream. They don't tell you being a weird musician is the dream. Diane is brave. I love her bravery. If I could be as brave as her, even for a minute, I might be a whole person, but I can't be. I'm not brave. I'm not. I cave in. I run to safety. She never runs to safety. She lives for danger and risk. She believed. I can't believe. I believe in nothing but my own safety and comfort. My whole life has been lived for comfort except for those few years with her. Now I am domestic. I have everything. I won. Look at me. The American sitcom dream my mother always dreamed of. She wrote a whole album about me. On her next album there were four songs about me, and her last album only contained one. Maybe it hurts to watch me disappear as her muse. Maybe being her muse is my one claim to fame in a world that loves fame. Maybe it is the one thing that provides me a sense of immortality. Maybe it is because I love it. Maybe I love being her muse.

THERESA: She wrote a whole album for you and you didn't even reach out?

TASHA: I wrote it off as mental illness. My friends told me she was a mentally ill bitch and we laughed about it. We laughed because we secretly knew she was a genius and we were just common, jealous bitches. I haven't even had sex with my wife in two years. We live here like roommates. I don't even think Ashley cares. She doesn't have strong emotions. I need that though, someone without strong emotions. I have strong emotions, and someone like Diane sends me into deep emotional places. I am also afraid of my emotions. I am afraid and worry all the time about how others perceive me. Diane was never like that. She never cared about what others thought of her. She only cared if her music made their hearts grow. (*Pause.*) Nothing in school prepares one for doing horrible things to other people and not being able to ever fix it. Nothing prepares you for years of one's life carrying around a secret pain. (*She yelled.*) Nothing prepares you to suffer silently for years. Diane has had to live the last seven years of her life wondering what she did wrong, not trusting anyone, wondering if I will knock on her door. I know she imagines it. I know she says my name at night. I know she can't forget. True love does not prevail. Comfort prevails. I am not a hero from a novel or play. I am the shitty sister who tells her sister who loves the stable boy that marrying money is the best thing to do. (*She yelled.*) I am a forgettable bitch. If I died tomorrow, Ashley would forget me. She would get therapy, practice yoga, and get over me in a year. She has no ability for nostalgia or being sentimental. She doesn't even have a favorite song. She would just go on. I have to lie to myself that Diane is a mentally ill person. It is the only path for me. I don't know why I am like this. I'm a normie. I'm a normal person. As each year passes into adulthood I become more and more bitter, just like my mother. I know my fate is to become a bitter old woman bitching about supermarket lines and idiot drivers. Hopefully I have enough money that my shitty attitude won't have any consequences. I would do anything to make Diane laugh again. I mean, think about it. (*She looked at Ryan and Theresa.*) People like Diane, who make great art, they are sad, tortured characters, not the type of people who laugh a lot. I would make her laugh, and out of this tormented soul a smile would come to her face, and she would look at me like I was the only person, the only fucking person, that could save her. Ashley has never looked at me like that once. If I was in the same room with Diane, and I made her laugh (*a smile cracked through the tears*), I would be happy. I would know life has meaning. I can't do that though. Please give her these things. Oh, the underwear. I should explain that. She used to put on my underwear and dance around saying, "Look, I'm Tasha, the most beautiful girl in the world." At the end of our relationship I told her she was full of bullshit, I'm not Rihanna. Every time she complimented me towards the end of our relationship I stopped her and told her she was full of bullshit, but she really believed it. She still believes it. She truly believes I am the most beautiful girl in the world. I did not believe it because I don't believe in anything except for my own comfort. When you meet Diane, remember that she believes in things. She isn't like us. She isn't weak. She isn't afraid of burning down everything for the sake of the dreams in her soul.

Chapter 16

On the road to Tucson, Arizona. Ryan drove and Theresa was tasked with researching Diane Butler, the acclaimed folk/country/punk musician. Theresa would read from interviews with Diane. In the interviews Theresa was articulate and thought provoking. She had a million opinions on music and on the state of affairs. People loved to interview her and get her opinions because she gave odd opinions that couldn't be categorized as right or left. It was easy to assume that she voted left, but sometimes she sounded like she believed in a weird freedom that didn't involve government participation. Additionally, her opinions contained spirituality. She had gone through a Buddhist phase that she loved talking about for a few years. When it ended she didn't go back to the person she was before. She was changed, but it wasn't part of her art anymore.

She was born in 1981 and grew up in West Texas, surrounded by country and western music. Her father played country music, predominantly Outlaw Country, George Jones, Willie Nelson, Emmylou Harris, Waylon Jennings, Johnny Cash, and Merle Haggard. Her grandfather got her her first guitar for Christmas when she was 10. It was actually one he just had hanging around, but he restrung it and gave it to her. Her dad and grandfather noticed she had perfect pitch. By the age of 15 she was playing in talent show competitions around West Texas. There was a video of a 14-year-old Diane Butler on Youtube playing Merle Haggard's "Mama Tried." Theresa and Ryan watched her play and were very impressed. When Diane got to high school she got into punk rock. She especially liked NOFX, and she also loved Pantera. As a fun intermezzo at her shows, she would take out her 1996 Dimebag Darrell guitar and play flashy solos. She called it "The Dimebag Intermezzo."

When she was eight years old her mother died of a drug overdose. Her mother was never around. Her father Ed took care of her. She had talked about this in an interview.

DIANE: You know, this is pretty common. Everyone has seen it. A child calls out for their mother, and the mom goes over and picks the child up, talks to the child. A child has something to show their mom, and even though the mom isn't interested at all, the mother listens and pretends they care. The thing is, I never had that. My mother never went near me. Two months after I was born, she gave me to my dad and just left. I have never known a mother's love, which is hard for several reasons: one, I didn't learn how to be a warm loving person, and two, a lot of social narratives in every society, on all the continents, depend upon the plot device of the loving mother. What if you don't have that? Then all social schemes, worked out over centuries, have no impact on your behavior. It is like I'm an accidental rebel.

Theresa read all that out loud.

THERESA: She has no mother. My mother has always been there for me. I mean, she says a lot of things that get on my nerves, but she's there. If you kicked me out of this car, right here, three hours from Las Vegas, I know one hundred percent I could call her and she would immediately get in her car and drive down here and pick me up. I know it one hundred percent.
RYAN: Mine too. That one hundred percent goes a long way, doesn't it?
THERESA: Yes. It is like I always know someone has my back.
RYAN: Maybe Diane's dad has her back.
THERESA: I hope so.

Diane's father moved to Tucson for a job in 2002. Diane went with him. They wanted a new life outside of West Texas. Diane attended the University of Arizona for music, where she learned jazz, classical guitar, and piano. There was a Youtube video of her playing Chopin's Op. 15, No. 1 in F major, Andante Cantabile on guitar in college. It had several thousand comments, 96% of them saying how beautiful it was.

Shortly after college, in 2005 when the Internet was starting to grow, she started making her own songs and posting them on Youtube. She created a blog where she talked about her days and music. She started to tour and meet people, gaining a reputation for making great music and being reliable and friendly. Several famous musicians had her open their shows.

Diane never became famous though. Her style of music could never compete with the bombastic rhythms of Rihanna or Beyonce. Her fans were derived from the Tegan and Sara and Ani DiFranco base, as well as people who grew up with country and western music but had broader tastes. She didn't mind this at all. Not one day of her life did she watch a Beyonce (Born the same year as her) video and think, "Why can't I be famous like Beyonce!" She never felt a sense of jealousy over other people's things.

THERESA: She doesn't feel jealousy over what other people have. I don't
    understand. She has no mother. Shouldn't she feel jealous?
RYAN: Maybe she learned at an early age that one can live without
    things.
THERESA: (*300 yard stare.*)

Diane didn't have the adoration of millions. She was just Diane Butler with her guitar.

Theresa played Diane's songs on an iPad. Ryan glanced over while he was driving to see a woman in an abandoned church playing the guitar and singing.

RYAN: It is really emotional.
THERESA: Yes. Like she is crying. There is a crying sound in her voice.
    Do you think this song is about Tasha? It is from 2015.
RYAN: That lines up with the timeline.
THERESA: I don't understand these two women. Tasha has everything,

but, like, it still seems like her life is ruined because she doesn't have one single thing.

RYAN: That one thing is big though.

THERESA: Yes. Who your spouse is determines how big your house is, where you live, what kind of car you drive. My mentor teaches us that our spouse is like a sun, and that everything orbits around that sun, and of course we are their sun. Who we choose to marry determines our success in the world. Our spouse can drive us to make more money or they can anchor us into a world of misery. Diane would anchor Tasha in a world of misery because they would never have a nice house in Summerlin or Anthem. Diane is the bad choice.

RYAN: You don't believe in true love, Theresa?

THERESA: (*This question made her mind go blank. She went to the void. There wasn't anything there. She didn't know what to answer.*) My mother has been divorced for many years. She has lived on her own taking care of me. Of course my dad has always supplied her with child support and money for me, but she has been alone. My mentor never mentions true love. He tells us that we need to dress well and work on good habits to succeed, and if we become hard working respectable people, then we will attract a hard working respectable person who will help us in life.

RYAN: Your mentor never mentions passion?

THERESA: My mentor tells us that we need to conserve our passion for our jobs, so that bosses know we want to get promoted and make more money.

RYAN: Did you ever think about true love?

THERESA: (*With no hesitation.*) I don't think so.

Theresa played a video of Diane singing at a honkey tonk in Nashville. The crowd was silent. When the song ended, the crowd screamed.

THERESA: I've never been exposed to music like this. These two women are so strange to me.

RYAN: Me neither. I went to college and studied law, then I worked in a law office for over a decade. I have been surrounded by people that cared nothing for the enjoyment of emotional exploration

THERESA: Emotional exploration?

RYAN: Like, they enjoy their emotions and moods, they feel fascinated by even great sadness, their emotions are strong and the only way to feel comfortable is to release it by music or literature or art. Their minds make sounds, then they have to make them a reality like it is their mission.

THERESA: Oh, I see. My family and friends don't do things like this. My cousin is a soundcloud rapper though. He makes rap songs, I never listen to them.

RYAN: That sounds cool.

THERESA: Mr. Neroni.

RYAN: Yes.

THERESA: Diane Butler scares me. She is, like, so passionate. She is college educated, she has thousands of likes on Youtube, thousands of friends on Twitter, and thousands of likes on Instagram. Her confidence is real, like she always had it. Even when she was a teenager she wasn't afraid of crowds and being herself. She has always been convinced that people wanted to hear her play the guitar. She never has doubt. I'm always full of doubt. My mentor tells me that if I create good habits my doubt will go away.

RYAN: She has doubts about love though. She has trust issues. Her music comes from these doubts about herself and from the life she has lived and still has to live. Her mother never loved her, so she makes art believing that if a lot of people adore her, then she is loved. But like you said, if you were kicked out of this car on the side of the highway right now, your mother for sure one hundred percent would come and pick you up. Diane knows none of her Instagram likes will pick her up. She will have to walk to the next stop alone.

THERESA: Oh, I see.

They arrived at Diane's small ranch house in south Tucson.

THERESA: It doesn't look like much.

RYAN: It is a small house, yes.

Ryan knocked on the door. Diane was not expecting them. An older man opened the door. His face was aged considerably, his body was tired, and his belly was swollen.

RYAN: We are here to see Diane We have a package for her.
OLDER MAN: (*In a west Texas accent.*) There are two people here to see you. (*He walked away at a slow pace.*)

A small woman stood up from the couch. She was watching Hilary Hahn's performance of Mendelssohn's Violin Concerto in E Minor op. 64. Diane looked at Ryan and Theresa. Her eyes were piecing and full of wonder.

DIANE: My father has cirrhosis of the liver. That's why he is swelled like that. He doesn't die. He keeps living. (*Pause.*) You have something for me. Let's go outside so I can smoke. I prefer talking to strangers while smoking.

Diane led them outside on a small patio with a tiny loveseat and two chairs. Diane sat in the loveseat with her legs stretched out on it. Theresa and Ryan took the chairs.

DIANE: Are you fans? What's up?
RYAN: No, we have a package for you.
DIANE: Oh, exciting. A package. (*She lit a cigarette.*)

Ryan took out a bag, the sunglasses and the pair of underwear in a zip lock bag, and placed them on the small table in front of Diane.
Diane looked at the items, staring silently, her eyes getting bigger. She immediately erupted into a full blown panic attack, hyperventilating, holding her chest.
Theresa did not move. She was frozen by the spectacle of emotion.
Ryan went to her father and asked what to do. He said to give her some water. He handed Ryan a bottle of water and he went outside.

Diane was still panicking.

The father came outside.

OLDER MAN: Give it ten minutes and she'll come back. (*He slowly walked away.*)

Ryan and Theresa sat for 10 minutes looking at her on the loveseat holding her chest and staring. Theresa remained frozen.

Then, suddenly:

DIANE: I'm okay. I'm back. It has been seven years. What could possibly be the point of this? She is married. I thought she had forgotten me. (*She sat up, lit another cigarette.*) I thought she had forgotten me. You know, people forget people all the time. I've dated a lot of people I've forgotten. I dated a woman named Sierra for a year. I never think about her. She never crosses my mind. I dated another person named Marissa. Marissa means nothing to me. And I wish both of them the best, you know. I thought Tasha had forgotten me, like I was nothing to her. And it killed me. But here are these two things. What did she say about me?

THERESA: She said she has thought of you every single day, but she has a nice house and a nice life, and she is too weak to leave it.

DIANE: But she remembers me?

THERESA: Yes, she remembers you. She loves you I think.

DIANE: (*Quietly.*) I want to write her off, you know, just make up some bullshit about how she is a dumb bitch, how she is horrible, how she is a cheating lying bitch and I could do better. That's what my friends told me to tell myself. I could never do it though. I have a very good memory. I can still play songs I learned twenty years ago. My mind can conjure Tasha and I's best moments, easily. Poof, I see them in my mind as if they were five minutes ago. It is dreadful to have a good memory. It is like a fucking curse. (*She looked at Ryan and Theresa.*) When you have a great memory for experiences, it is like time doesn't exist and you are all the times at once. Blessed are the forgetful.

THERESA: What do you mean, great memory for experiences?
DIANE: I can recall events from twenty-five years ago, what everyone was wearing, what the weather was like, what everyone said. It is like a playback.
THERESA: Wow, that is so cool.
DIANE: (*She looked at Theresa.*) (*This person doesn't understand what I'm trying to articulate.*) (*She looked at Ryan.*) (*He understands, but doesn't have the same problem. He has other problems. Both of them are trying to be friendly.*) It helps sometimes. So, since our relationship ended, I've put out three albums. I've traveled the world. I've been to Europe, Asia, and South America. When I go on tour everyone is so nice to me. They treat me like a queen. I sit in a chair and people get my coffee. I get free meals. Important, amazing people want to eat dinner and drink beer with me. I accomplished everything I wanted. I mean, to you normie folk I'm not famous like Beyonce, but when I was a teenager I had a dream of the perfect songs. In my mind I could see the songs that would perfectly express what it meant to be human for me. I didn't have the skills to create those songs, but I knew if I learned everything I could about the guitar and singing I could, one day, make those songs, and I did. I made those songs, and people liked them. It was the songs that were the dream, not the fame. The songs. I had a vision and I executed. What I did not know was that it would require a muse, and that the muse in question would not be around for any of my accomplishments. I stood in Paris, London, Tokyo, Seoul, Valparaiso, and Buenos Aires, and she was not there. I couldn't stop thinking every time, "Tasha would love this." Then, that very night, a strange woman would want to have sex with me, and I would do it. I don't know if this is real though. Maybe it is all mental illness. Maybe I've lost my mind, but I am still capable of performing tasks that resemble normal human behavior, like driving a car and eating. I mean, there are a lot of crazy people who can perform basic functional tasks. Maybe I am just one of them. There is nothing I can do to fix this. My mind won't let me forget. My mind won't just move onto new things. It won't let me. For seven years I've gone to sleep every night hoping tomorrow will be the day that

it forgets her, but at some point, at some random point, it thinks of her again. The problem is that it is bearable. I can endure it. There is a part of me that enjoys it. (*Pause.*) I'm happy she did this. It was nice of her. (*She picked up the underwear, took them out of the package.*) Did she tell you why she gave these to me?

RYAN: Yes, it sounded cute.

DIANE: I was cute once. (*She smiled a little.*) I'll play you a song. You wanna hear a song?

They went inside the house. Diane sat at an old upright piano.

DIANE: It is old but it works. I tune it myself.

Theresa and Ryan stood a few feet away, but within seeing distance of her hands.

DIANE: I'm going to play "Always on my Mind" by Willie Nelson, but Elvis did a great version too.

She began to play.

Chapter 17

The next mission was in mid-December, 2019, at the Grand Canyon Caverns, north of I-40, on the way to the South Rim. It was in the middle of nowhere. There was no 4G or Internet. It was a beautiful land, endless in all directions, not as barren of fauna as Las Vegas, greener. When the sunset happened, you knew you were on the edge of the world.

Theresa and Ryan parked the Honda Civic Type R in front of the restaurant that contained the elevator that went 200 feet below into the driest caves in North America. Not a drop of water. Still to this day, no one knows where the oxygen came from in the cave.

Above the cave was a restaurant and souvenir shop. It was Ryan and Theresa's mission to go into the restaurant and find Dr. Benway. Dr. Benway had contacted Ryan with a new mission. Dr. Benway did not explain the mission, only that it required meeting at the Grand Canyon Caverns.

Ryan and Theresa went into the restaurant and looked around. It looked like an old west movie, everything wooden, a carved bear, cowboy nostalgia all over the walls. Ryan loved old wooden places in the middle of nowhere. The more desolate they were, the more he loved them. Theresa didn't know what to make of it. She liked fast food and never ate at nice places. She had never even had sushi or been to a vegan restaurant.

Dr. Benway waved his hand so Ryan could see. Ryan and Theresa went over to sit. They sat on the same side of the booth facing Dr. Benway.

DR. BENWAY: Is this Theresa?

RYAN: Yes, my assistant.

DR. BENWAY: (*To Theresa.*) I'm going to say this, and it will sound harsh, but I have to say it for legal reasons: What you will see today will be very odd. Actually, super odd. This is probably going to be the weirdest day of your life. Are you okay with that?

THERESA: (*I am nervous. Don't show nervousness. Show confidence.*) I'm ready. (*That's not true, you aren't ready for anything. You have never been ready in your entire life. Is this how things happen? By saying yes even though you don't know what is going to happen?*)

DR. BENWAY: Another thing, if you tell anyone what you saw today agents from the United States Government will hunt you down and kill you. Please understand that in life we can have amazing experiences if we follow orders. Do you understand?

THERESA: Yes, I understand. (*Okay, I can't tell anyone ever. Not even my mom. I won't even tell my mom. This is how you become a success, by following orders. I feel nervous.*)

RYAN: How is Randall Flagg?

DR. BENWAY: He is still sleeping. No movement, blood pressure normal. You know what though? Mel took that lightsaber emotion thing away from me. I kept shooting myself with it instead of working. Fucking Mel. She said they didn't know the long term side-effects yet. I yelled "Let me die, Mel." She said I was the property of the United States Government and I could not die; I worked for all three hundred and thirty million people and I had a duty to the history of America and democracy to remain alive and not be a lightsaber emotion thing addict. I didn't agree with any of this, but she had a gun and took it away.

RYAN: (*That was weird.*)

THERESA: (*I have no idea what he is talking about. Should I know? Should I be asking questions? My mentor said that asking appropriate questions shows that I am listening and people will think I'm smart. Who is Mel? Do I know Mel?*)

DR. BENWAY: The thing in the cave that I will show you is called Conjecture Head. It is a large disembodied head that only speaks in conjecture.

THERESA: (*What is con-jek-shure?*)

DR. BENWAY: We do not know when Conjecture Head showed up. A psychic medium was taking a cave tour one day, just for fun, with their family, and they told us, "There's a giant head down there yelling conjecture endlessly." Of course, we had to check this out. We have these special helmets to see ghosts. We tried to sell it to Apple and other places. Nobody wanted it. It tested horribly in Focus Groups. You will obviously have the helmets on when meeting Conjecture Head.

RYAN: It is a head that only speaks in conjecture?

DR. BENWAY: Yes, only conjecture. Blanket generalizations, logical fallacies, and a perverted disregard for facts. Conjecture Head hates empathy, logic, facts, and statistics.

RYAN: Can we talk to Conjecture Head?

DR. BENWAY: No, Conjecture Head never stops talking. We have yelled at it, thrown rocks at it, shot it with water, nothing happens. The rocks and water just go right through him. It is like he is there, but not there. He only appears to two senses, sight and sound. Whatever it is does not appeal to smell, taste and touch.

RYAN: I feel really excited for this.

DR. BENWAY: I knew you would.

THERESA: (*I am nervous, what does dis-meme-bod-deed mean?*)

DR. BENWAY: You two have been selected for this because you two have no real opinions. It is like you two have nothing to do with the world. The world exists, but you have no concern for it. For example, Theresa has never even voted.

THERESA: No, I haven't.

DR. BENWAY: Attorney Neroni here has voted three times in his whole adult life.

RYAN: Yes.

DR. BENWAY: Here's a question, what do you think about Donald Trump?

RYAN: I do not prefer his policies, but one day his career as president will end.

THERESA: I do not...

DR. BENWAY: You are afraid to answer because you don't know my political party? And when you are around people with college degrees, you get very nervous, because your mind explodes us into super important people?

THERESA: Yes. (*This is painful.*)

DR. BENWAY: I'm just like you Theresa.

THERESA: (*Why is he focusing on me?*)

DR. BENWAY: Lonely. Are you lonely Theresa?

THERESA: (*No has ever asked me such a question.*) I am.

DR. BENWAY: We must go now. The helmets are downstairs.

They got into the elevator at the back of the building. The door closed and Dr. Benway pressed the button to go down.

THERESA: I've never been in a cave.

DR. BENWAY: It is pretty cool. I love caves. I've been to Mammoth and Carlsbad. I'm a great lover of caves... Oh, here are flashlights. It is pitch black down there.

Dr. Benway handed the flashlights over to Ryan and Theresa. Theresa held the flashlight, clicking it on to see if it worked. Ryan did not check. He seemed unconcerned about what was happening. He didn't seem to be thinking. He was just existing.

The elevator doors opened. They left the elevator. It was blackness. They turned on their flashlights and proceeded into the cave.

DR. BENWAY: It isn't far.

As they walked, Ryan and Theresa looked around at the cave. They both thought it was neat.

DR. BENWAY: Here we are. Exciting right?

RYAN: I feel pretty excited. How about you Theresa?

THERESA: Yes, I am happy to be here. (*Was that the right thing to say?*)

Dr. Benway retrieved a box from behind a rock and took out two helmets. They looked like helicopter helmets, a giant shaded covering for the eyes, like a bug. He handed them to Ryan and Theresa. They held them in their hands, looking at them.

DR. BENWAY: Put them on your heads.

They put the helmets on. Dr. Benway clicked on buttons on the helmets. The helmets had a little green light that shined when they were operational.

DR. BENWAY: Look at you two. You look like bugs.
RYAN: I am Gregor Samsa.
DR. BENWAY: Good joke Attorney Neroni. Keep them coming.
THERESA: (*This thing is heavy.*)
RYAN: Oh my God. What is that yelling?
THERESA: I hear it too.

Dr. Benway positioned their bodies so they could see Conjecture Head.

RYAN: It is a giant head yelling.
THERESA: This is terrifying. What the fuck is that?
RYAN: I've never heard you swear before, Theresa.
THERESA: There's a giant head Ryan!
RYAN: Okay, let's calm ourselves. Take a deep breath. Your heart is probably beating fast. Let it calm. Don't fight it. Just let it happen. Your heart will calm itself.

Theresa took a deep breath. She felt her heart beating rapidly, but did not fight it. She stood there staring at Conjecture Head. After a minute her heart rate went down and she was able to listen to Conjecture Head.

Ryan and Theresa listened:

CONJECTURE HEAD: (*In a yelling voice.*) I am the almighty Conjecture Head I know everything everything is known by me burn it all down whatever my head tells me is true my head has an interior narrative all of which that narrative says is true my head contains all truths i only know my experience my experience is the best experience i am forgetful of my own experiences my personal opinion can be verified by my personal experience which is the only experience which is the only opinion i have all the opinions i am good at one thing therefore i am entitled to comment on all things i never make opinions based on my personal emotions and not objective reality i have tradition on my side i have empathy on my side i have god on my side i have my religion i have my political party i have my television shows i have my music i have my favorites i do not like oranges all those who like oranges are gross all oranges are gross this is my theory of justice this is my epistmology i know that i know that i know through conflation i make the best youtube videos and twitter comment cancellations i write you do you and prove points to get taxes reduced in federal state and local governments my head notifies me of self-evident speculation my head takes in information it feels it if it likes it it takes it and if it does not like it does not take it i feel good about who i am in relationship to my friends and society what about this he is a piece of shit anyway all liberals are stupid they are all vegan and want to destroy cheeseburgers all republicans are fascist racist and hate women i have a raging hard-on orgasm when i can feel self-righteous i go to church therefore i have the high moral ground i am liberal and believe in national healthcare i have the moral highgound in marianas trench from the moral highground i kill anakin win all awards i go to sleep happy i told my uncle he killed all the native americans and enslaved every black person uncle time if it wasn't for the insert race i woundn't have to everything is me everyone is me a world of mes that do not agree with me i have never donated to anything i voted for bernie i voted for nader npr voice if it wasn't for insert random historical incidents i would be have had unmarried sex with forty people still moral highground i don't pay my employees a livable wage still moral highground i told my gay son to kill himself still moral highground i call millions of people stupid still moral highground if they were me then they would feel wonderful and do the right things all the time i hate country music i hate rap david lynch i am so sad christo died i didn't get anything because of privilege i don't have privilege i went to a protest i have never volunteered in my life that was not required for a class i yell at people in bars i yell at my children because they don't want to be me i notify the cashier that she is mexican i notify everyone that all liberals are babies while i am yelling i kick over a garbage can in oregon at a protest then i win all the awards i have beliefs the best beliefs easy beliefs like abortion is bad black lives matter abortion is bad and black lives do matter but other beliefs regarding wages and global warming and poverty too complex time consuming you can believe in those things unless you put effort into them let the christians help the poor i hate christians i hate pedophile catholics i love hispanics i want america to be a better place except for the people i don't like i can't control politicans i cannot control people that are not me i don't know how science works i don't know how statistics work i cannot name one federal agency i read books by an old boomer that tell me that american white people are so intelligent and quick witted that they can manipulate any other group of people into destroying themselves i am not racist i am not racist women should be respected women have periods there are women that they do not have periods but are actually women all the way or no way no grey areas joe rogan interviews jordan peterson i have to have an opinion i can never just listen and love believe in basic dignity and the rule of law leave it at that have to make a big deal of everything nobody is a person first i rate people's personness based upon a scale that has me at cartesian zero i was in the military therefore everyone should shut the fuck up need to yell yelling is my personality through anger i verify my results i do not believe people who are not angry anger can revise history anger can make $1 + 1 + 3$ anger verifies carbon emisions $1 + N = 3$ N is my discomfort level habit changes asking me to do things liberal tard asses fascist republicans non voting scum everyone who doesn't vote should cut off their heads i've replaced the entire history of humanity with me screaming on the internet i don't believe in trials i don't believe in civil law i believe in prisons and lower taxes giant militaries and lower taxes national health care free college universal basic income and lower taxes there is no truth i have a had a job for thirty years i worked forty hours a week i took shit from my boss there was no truth in that i made it through life i am entitled to my opinion verification anger i am twenty-two years i grew up in a mcmansion in the suburbs i too have an opinion i am not scamming you i have opinions regarding long dead people and their habits i yell i win all arguments i have purple hair verification tattoos i don't like people they are not me this is the issue judge everyone else is not me i believe in an america where everyone wants to be me everyone becomes me where everyone concedes and then clones themselves into me i am the ultimate individual i am alone in a vast landscape of right to work employment news media run by people who are all ultimate individuals i am the sun everyone and everything orbits around me solipsism is real i prove it i contain all proofs all i have to do is recall my personal experiences and there the answer presents itself everything the government does is a hoax even the post office hoax DMV hoax roads hoax i do not know where roads come from i know everything and it feels great the government should fix my incel jaw line or provide me a wife i am vaginal hat my okcupid reads unless you make eighty thousand dollars a year and have a new car please do not call me i do not go near poor people i know what should be done with poor people there are many different types of poor people they are all black and hispanic poor asians don't exist the people who serve my food at the orange chicken place are not actually poor but nyu graduates white poor people say things i disagree with therefore i operate in a way where they don't exist either let the christians feed them on thanksgiving i hate christians stupid fucks all homos go to hell why won't my children go to chuch why do i have to yell so much oh it is because you are stupid and won't listen i base my opinions on my friends facial reactions i go to my

friend's house we bust open a can budweiser/ipa i say something
that sounds good inside my head ultimate verification machine my
head the great head that is my head my friend looks happy insert
racist comment insert liberal virtues everyone does this and we
don't obviously we don't do that because we are great even though
we do it all the time my friends do it all the time i do the me things
all the time all the time i am me and i'm great my head notifies me
my head has jurisdiction over all existence my head requires no outside input it is the input machine that puts itself inside of itself itself feeds itself my friend's facial and inflections are good enough i
know this is true because it is getting me tenure i know this is true
because my dad didn't contradict me when i said it justice depends
upon me there is no need for trials or democracy or procedure or
signing stupid documents or waiting in line phone calls being put on
hold society could run efficiently if they just hooked up the entire
world to my head my head could run the entire system through
self-importance a greater world will be made through fear discomfort scamming and self-projection virture is created a better world
where everyone is happy i do not believe in god i do not believe in
the government i do not want to pay taxes schools are stupid basing
all of one's opinions on feelings i am the answer you are seeking
plato aristotle st. thomas aquinas confucius mencius the torah the
new testament the koran the teachings of buddha zen masters no
use to me i grew up on entertainment the television is the pulse of
the people i was raised by people that watched mork and mindy and
happy days i was raised on growing pains and friends saint augustine
knew nothing of tv locke hegel marx wittgenstein sartre de beauvoir
camus postmodernists sorbonne latin american dictators old black
lady who has been through every trouble imaginable still smiles at
strangers a mexican/honduran/salvadoran man who did the impossible to get his wife and kids across the border I have replaced the
entire history of europe bach mozart all the saints popes kings
queen peasants italian french architecture italian art french art kant
pascal chopin replaced with blue lives matter white people eat may-
onnaise memes veganism yeast sandwiches public intellectuals de-

bating the merits of oscar awarding movies i hold nothing dear only through money clout likes followers do i live a great life god is dead bring on the memes i do not want people to find peace i want everyone to be a gay preacher wealth worshipping commie through self-help platitudes the world writes a new story every day driving in my truck wearing sunglasses you don't really win a million dollars the government comes and steals it i give you the solutions listen to my yelling i have a podcast amy goodman radcliffe harvard grad angry i am the great head i have the answers the entertainment you need i will feed you the anger the hate the unfriendliness you need to make it through life fill your spirit full of distrust reactionary vitriol despair alienation create alienation where there is none grow the alienation make it stronger generalize needlessly disregard statistics correlation multiple regression analysis live your best life you do you comment viciously blame insert group give fault find anyone anywhere and blame them believe life should be perfect never have a perfect just get angry about little things your soul doesn't need love you don't need to worry about other people that don't look like you make needless comments the more needless the more perfect your needless comments if you don't have anything to say call them fat call people sheep call them fascists call them any name that might hurt them except specific words that are considered hurtful because of historical reasons cancel grandma she isn't stupid stuck in the language of the past she is a murderer and you aren't being annoying you are being a great person burn it all down on facebook while eating flaming hot cheetos i am the world i am the great head all i know is that i know everything i am the anger inside you i promise i will grow that anger until you become an ultimate individual who agrees completely with their friend group help me make money let's conflate

Dr. Benway tapped Ryan and Theresa on the shoulder. They removed the helmets.

RYAN: It never stops?

DR. BENWAY: Never.

THERESA: That was horrible. That was the scariest thing I've ever seen. I didn't understand anything it said. (*Facial expression showing shock and despair.*)

DR. BENWAY: How did it make you feel, Theresa?

THERESA: I feel in pain.

Dr. Benway, Ryan, and Theresa went back to the restaurant. Dr. Benway gave them questionnaires to fill out on their experiences. Ryan and Theresa completed the surveys. Dr. Benway said they were for research to better understand Conjecture Head.

Dr. Benway then told them their next mission was to go to Salt Lake City and meet a man at a restaurant called Cafe Shambala.

Chapter 18

Ryan and Theresa were traveling north on I-15 to Salt Lake City. There had been silence for an hour. Theresa was staring out the window. Ryan quietly drove. A George Strait greatest hits CD Ryan had bought at a Cracker Barrel in Kingman, Arizona played on the stereo.

Theresa looked in Ryan's direction.

THERESA: I don't get it. You were an attorney. You were successful. You had respect. You had power, and you just threw it away. I don't get it.

RYAN: (*Looking forward.*) Why do you want to know. What's your intention?

THERESA: You just threw it away.

RYAN: (*I don't want to say anything that would destroy our relationship. The truth doesn't matter. There isn't any necessity to this. Maybe this is me, ignoring people again. Just tell her. We are trapped in this car for another three hours. What is the worst that could happen?*)

THERESA: I just wonder. (*Her eyes, friendly.*)

RYAN: (*I don't trust the validity of my own emotions. How can I trust giving them to someone else?*) I didn't believe anymore.

THERESA: What is there to believe in? You were successful.

RYAN: One day I was in the office. All the support staff were there, the paralegals, assistants, the people who order medical records, the scanner people, and the receptionist. It was some kind of meeting, and one of the lawyers told everyone that he had saved enough money that his kids—I think he had three—could all go to Yale or Harvard if they wanted, and they would have no debt when they graduated.

THERESA: Oh, that's great. What a good dad.

RYAN: He saved that money by paying the support staff unlivable wages. The place I worked paid the scanner people ten dollars an hour, the receptionist twelve dollars, maybe four people even made twenty dollars an hour. We made enough money that we could have given them livable wages where they could have bought houses, had at least new Nissans, and taken nice vacations. Instead we paid them as little as possible because we knew we could get away with it. I didn't feel that important. I didn't feel that entitled. I didn't feel like I had a right to take people's money and kiss my own ass.

THERESA: You are the lawyer though.

RYAN: I couldn't be a lawyer without those workers. Those workers are essential for me to do my job... (*Pause.*) This isn't about politics either. This isn't, like, even me wanting a better world. This is me, just me, feeling that I can't do this. I don't understand why we as a people are so focused on wealth. The best things that happen in life are having a safe place to sleep, good food, family, dancing, and music. A lower-level, less destructive world could be created and still supply us with dental care. We aren't obsessed with worlds we could make, but with people and what they are doing all the time, like we have all become shit-talkers. Shit talking is not an answer politically or for the soul. I am worried about other things, I guess. I worked with people for years. They worked within twenty feet of me, and I completely ignored them as people. I failed to bother with them as people. It never occurred to me to even care about their lives. I didn't feel like a person. People get to know each other. They have relationships. I was more worried about my car and hair than any of the humans that were around me.

THERESA: (*Why does this man want to be my friend?*)

RYAN: Life becomes cheap when we treat each other as disposable, when we pay each other the lowest prices. Instead of deeply thinking about the lives of our employees and their wants and needs, the main calculations are our house, our car, our vacations, our kids' college educations. Those are the main considerations when determining wages, not their lives, not what they need. I am sickened with myself. I am appalled by the monster I was, and this villainy is adored by the general population, millions of people pleading to be slaves, to have their lives made worse by the people they trust. I hate to use the word "slaves," but we are so in love with this form of injustice, we can't even make a name for it. I mean, what are you, Theresa? You grew up poor with non-English speaking parents that didn't get their citizenship for years after being here. You work part time at Ross. They won't let you get full time to get health insurance. Do you even have health insurance?

THERESA: Obamacare.

RYAN: Well, at least you have that... When people become disposable, it is only a matter of time before we view each other's deaths as meaningless. Hierarchical thinking leads to the allowance of death. You are no longer a person, but a thing in a hierarchy. Nothing remains but levels of importance, which inevitably leads to corruption and scamming, everyone else being seen as a threat, or just annoying. Those in authority become cynical because they know what they are doing to gain and retain power, and those deemed unimportant lose hope and become cynical, shit-happens type people: "Who cares? I have to live as an unimportant person, so who cares if someone else dies, if someone else is sick, if someone else is deprived of something they need?" This situation leads to cannibalism in the low-born, fighting over scarce resources, each year going deeper into their cynicism, never knowing dignity. They have lost nothing.

THERESA: (*She put her hand on Ryan's shoulder.*) I like you.

RYAN: You like me?

THERESA: I'll be your friend.

RYAN: I appreciate that. I'll be your friend too.

Chapter 19

They sat in the Shambala Cafe across from a big man named Elder Ted Anderson. Ted was a big man and Mormon-looking. He wore a nice white and grey suit. Who he was, what job he held, no information was provided about what status Mr. Anderson held in this world. Ryan assumed he was part of Area 51, but did not inquire. Ryan and even Theresa had begun to enjoy this new world they had entered.

Ted sat across from Ryan and Theresa.

TED: I like this place, I hope you find something you like.

RYAN: It looks really nice in here.

TED: It's pretty Buddhist, but still has Christmas decorations, I like that.

RYAN: Yeah, totally.

THERESA: I've never eaten food like this.

TED: Well, it will be a surprise then. This is what I have to offer you. We like what you two do. We've been watching you these last several months. Both of you can keep a secret, and you work well together. Theresa has been a huge surprise to us. She faces her fears and does what needs to be done. I think (*looking at Theresa*) you are one of those people that just needed to be given a chance in life. Your life didn't offer the type of chances required for you to shine. We believe you contain the abilities to work with Mr. Neroni and achieve great results. We want to set the both of you up in Tonopah. We will provide you both housing, a small law office as a cover, and a salary.

RYAN: Will Theresa have a living wage? Will her wage be similar to mine?

TED: Would you like that Mr. Neroni?

RYAN: That is all I want.

TED: Okay, we will set that up.

    Theresa smiled.

TED: Your life will be in the desert now. We will provide you with weapons training and even faster cars.

RYAN: That sounds nice.

TED: (*Looking serious.*) This is not a United States Federal government institution. We are the Committee. We provide safety and security to the mobility of objects.

THERESA: Even like the sunglasses and underwear we brought to someone?

TED: Especially those objects. There is no higher priority than items shared between two families or ex-lovers. One time, someone in West Virginia found old poems written by the previous owner of the house they lived in, somebody's grandpa. We found the granddaughter and asked her if she wanted them, and we transported them to her. There is nothing more precious to us than a poem written by a grandpa.

RYAN: This sounds good.

TED: What about you Theresa? Do you want to do it?

THERESA: Yes.

Chapter 20

On January 4th, 2020, Dr. Benway was on the bed in the Venetian watching Randall Flagg. He had still not moved, but Dr. Benway did his duty and checked on him everyday. The new year had come. The unemployment rate was 3.4%. People had fallen in love with Baby Yoda. Everything was going well. It was going to be an election year, which was always bumpy, but that's democracy.

Dr. Benway received a text message from Mel.

MEL: Look at this tweet. You think it is anything? Do we need to worry?

TWEET: World Health Organization: #China has reported to WHO a cluster of #pneumonia cases - with no deaths - in Wuhan, Hubei Province. Investigations are underway to identify the cause of this illness.

DR. BENWAY: (*Texting back.*) No, probably like SARS and Swine Flu. Those never did anything.

Dr. Benway laid on the bed staring at the ceiling. Then he heard a voice.

MR. FLAGG: Hello, Dr. Benway.

Dr. Benway sat up and looked at the unknown man. The man was looking directly at him with a small grin.

MR. FLAGG: Dr. Benway, thank you for taking care of me, I deeply appreciate it. (*He stood up, fixed his suit and tie, then walked out of the hotel room.*)

DR. BENWAY: (*Texting Mel.*) On second thought, we might need to worry.

Acknowledgements

Ryan Rowland, Rudy Hinton, Nate Perkins, Jorge Alejandro Prado Vargas, Adrián Martínez, Jesús Carmona-Robles, Soeun Seo, Sandra Buenaventura, Jorge Núñez Riquelme, Oliver Zärandi, Brian Alan Ellis, Fernando E. Chávez Finol, and IRL friends, Nicholas Chiarella, Oma Mullins, Jake Levine, Fatima Askaryar, Stephanie Sumler, Cheyne Shirley, Mina Myers, and Vi Khi Nao.

About the Author

Noah Cicero was born in 1980 in a field in Northeast, Ohio. He grew up in a small town with one stoplight. He has worked at restaurants and grocery stores. He attended Youngstown State University for Political Science and the College of Southern Nevada for Paralegal Studies. He currently works in litigation. Noah Cicero has a deep love for the judicial system. If you ever sit with him drinking a beer, he is just as likely to talk about Modernist novels as he is regarding how Civil Litigation works. He has taken part in seven trials, something he is proud of, exclusive of writing. He has approximately 10 books published and over half have been translated in several languages. He has done four international speaking engagements in Mexico, Chile, Peru and South Korea. He has lived in South Korea teaching ESL; the Grand Canyon twice as a dishwasher and cashier; Oregon twice, both times as a shiftless person; and has been living in Las Vegas, Nevada since 2013. He hikes every Sunday. He has been to the bottom of the Grand Canyon four times.

Sixty Tattoos I Secretly Gave Myself at Work
by Tanner Ballengee

Ex-girlfriends. LSD. Motorcyle and canoe trips. *Seinfeld.* Skateboarding. Drunk friends and punk rock and shitty jobs. *Sixty Tattoos I Secretly Gave Myself at Work* is the most beautiful, the most vulnerable of punk and adventure memoirs. Each vignette centers around a hand-poked tattoo that the author gave himself on company time.

The Pocket Peter Kropotkin

Collected in this cute, pocket-sized volume are eight of Kropotkin's essays. The book starts with his indispensable article on anarchism, originally written for the Eleventh Edition of the *Encyclopedia Britannica,* and moves forward to expound on his ides, which include prison abolition, syndicalism, expropriation, etc.

The Pocket Emma Goldman

Some great Goldman essays collected in one place. This book is perfect for carrying in your pocket so you can secretly read anarcha-feminist literature while you're supposed to be working.

The Silence is the Noise
by Bart Schaneman

After a few years living in cities, Ethan Thomas returns to his rural Nebraska hometown and takes a reporting job at the community newspaper. He stumbles upon a big story when an out-of-state oil company pumps enough fracking wasewater into the ground to induce earthquakes. As Ethan learns to write he reconnects with a young woman from his childhood. This is a story about the complicated relationship we have with the places we know best, the pull of the ouside world, and finding something to love.

The Pocket Aleister Crowley

Famously called "the most evil man in Britain," Aleister Crowley's impact upon the occult traditions was nothing short of monumental. The selected works contained within this pocket-sized volume offer a way of thinking that is scientific and individualistic, but also deeply mythic and metaphysical, leaving room for both human intelligence and religious inspiration.

Propaganda of the Deed:
The Pocket Alexander Berkman

It was July 23, 1892, and Alexander Berkman was planning to die. He just had some business to attend to first. Dressed in a new suit and black derby hat, Berkman burst into the Pittsburg office of Henry Clay Frick, the notoriously anti-union manager of the Carnegie Steel Company. From his pocket, Berkman produced a pistol.

This pocket-sized book collects the shorter works of on of the world's most influential anarchists.

The Soul of Man Under Socialism
by Oscar Wilde

"Socialism, Communism, or whatever one chooses to call it, by converting private property into public wealth, and substituting co-operation for competition, will restore society to its proper condition of a thoroughly healthy organism, and insure the material well-being of each member of the community."

Los Espiritus
by Josh Hyde

Four grandmas stop the passing of generational karma by interrupting a wedding with a funeral. *Los Espiritus* is an absurdist, spiritual romantic comedy with a heartfelt message: "How do we transcend our humanity?"

America At Play
by Mathias Svalina

America At Play is a collection of instructions for children's games. Part poetry, part whimsy, part despair, games such as "Freight Train Tag," "Baptism," and "World War" teach valuable lessons, such as how to play and how to be American. It is, Herclitus said, reality's nature to remain hidden, but its rules are easily observed.

The Pocket Austin Osman Spare

Working on the cutting edge of both magic and art, Austin Osman Spare developed a unique synthesis of older ritual magic systems with post-modern, erotic, and surrealist themes. His theory of magic eschews complex formula and ritual to favor creativity, spontaneity, and ecstasy, embracing artistic expression and alternative sexualities.

With a Difference
by Francis Daulerio and Nick Gregorio

Cowritten by poet Francis Daulerio and fiction writer Nick Gregorio, With a Difference is inspired in part by Rancid and NOFX's 2002 BYO split cover album. Gregorio has adapted 10 of Daulerio's poems into stories, and Daulerio has turned 10 of Gregorio's stories into poems. Like a vinyl record, the book must be flipped over to read both "sides."

Western Erotica Ho
by Bram Riddlebarger

Western Erotica Ho follows the author on a family camping vacation from Ohio to Wyoming and back while the Summer Olympics filter through news headlines across the country, and the Sturgis Bike Rally inn South Dakota draws thousands of bikers to the Black Hills.

www.tridentcafe.com/trident-press